SUSAN MILLS
WILSON

MELTDOWN

A Romantic Suspense Novel

ISBN: 978-0-9911691-2-2

This novel is dedicated to the memory of soldiers and law enforcement officers who have made the ultimate sacrifice to protect the rights and freedom of citizens.

Also by Susan Mills Wilson

GOOD GONE BAD

HER LYING EYES

ACKNOWLEDGEMENTS

My sincere gratitude to the following persons who supported me and helped make the publication of this book possible.

First of all, I want to thank my husband for his love and support. Before anyone sees my work, he is the first to delve into my story. My gratitude to my son, David, my daughter, Christina, and my twin, Donna, who have always believed in me.

I am forever grateful to my editor, Christie Stratos of Proof Positive, for her careful scrutiny to details. She puts the extra coat of polish on the final product.

A special thanks to my book designer, Mindy Kuhn of Blue Butterfly Creative, who makes my book covers standout with her beautiful graphic design. Also for her layout skills.

To my writer friends in the Mystery Critique Group. I appreciate their help in shaping the story and characters. They kept me on track and from going off the deep-end. Dennis, Reita, Susan, and Jim, thank you for your counsel, encouragement, and friendship.

Special thanks to the officers and personnel of the Citizens Academy for: Charlotte-Mecklenburg Sheriff's Office, Matthews Police Department, and Charlotte-Mecklenburg Police Department. Their many hours of instruction and demonstrations gave me a deeper understanding and a greater appreciation of law enforcement.

Last of all, I want to thank my readers. Without you, what would be the point?

OLD WAR DREAMS

By Walt Whitman

In midnight sleep of many a face of anguish,
Of the look at first of the mortally wounded, (of that
indescribable look,)
Of the dead on their backs with arms extended wide,
I dream, I dream, I dream.

Of scenes of Nature, fields and mountains,
Of skies so beauteous after a storm, and at night the moon so
unearthly bright,
Shining sweetly, shining down, where we dig the trenches and
gather the heaps,
I dream, I dream, I dream.

Long have they pass'd, faces and trenches and fields,
Where through the carnage I moved with a callous
composure, or away from the fallen,
Onward I sped at the time — but now of their forms at night,
I dream, I dream, I dream.

CHAPTER ONE
DAY ONE - FRIDAY, JULY 4, 2014

A low fog hugged the base of the trees like a child with its arms around its mother. As if some hardy soul might be up before dawn on a holiday weekend, Jared Bolten slunk around in the cover of darkness. Loaded down with his rucksack and rifle case, he made the trek to the church bell tower, a cakewalk compared to the hikes he'd made as a sniper specialist in Iraq and Afghanistan. He was in a different war now, dressed the part in camo, his face smeared with matching paint. He wore hiking boots and his favorite baseball cap turned backwards. His duty belt held two extra mags of ammo, a hunting knife, range finder, and a flash drive. The coil of thick rope hooked to his belt swung with each step he took.

He left his cell phone and survival kit back in his truck awaiting his return, which had to be quick. So quick, he had practiced the sprint from the tower back to the isolated wooded area. According to his stopwatch, he could make the trip in five minutes flat. If anyone got in his way, he had his .45 Glock locked and loaded at his side. One shot center mass should stop them cold. Once he ran back to his truck, he'd have to gun the engine to get the hell out of there and to the main highway, where he hoped to blend in with traffic. Of course, he'd have to wipe all the gunk off his face and sport a different hat, his black cowboy with the wide brim. He called it his lucky hat because he'd worn it to a bar where he'd met a hot blonde, drunk and ready for him. They did it all night long.

He had long spidery legs, and like his arms, they were all muscle. He could eat junk food, drink beer, smoke an occasional joint and still stay fit. You don't get flabby being a brick mason, working from six to six every damn day. But those days were behind him. He'd never lift another crummy brick for as long as he lived. After today, his life would never be the same. His name would be plastered on every newspaper around the country. Hell, maybe overseas. His manifesto would go viral. His message would be out, and no one—not one fucking soul—could ignore him. They'd lap up every word he'd written, and they couldn't dispute one word of it. It was the truth, as God was his witness.

§

Five hours later... Showtime. Jared's heart raced. He felt beads of sweat run down his neck and forehead. To calm himself, he took deep breaths and bent his head backwards and then from side to side until his neck bone popped.

He was pleased to see no obstruction in the crosshairs of his scope. There were no trees within the firing range. Instead two soccer fields were straight ahead. Beyond that and across the narrow street was the park where the festivities were in full swing. A smorgasbord of targets packed in close, a sniper's wet dream. He figured he could get off twenty shots easy every minute that he fired.

Earlier, waiting for the first band to take the stage, he had spread a drop cloth to cover the perimeter. Then he set up the Remington 700 bolt-action rifle on the ledge of the tower. From the rucksack, he pulled out a throw rag. Similar to a netted laundry bag, it was dyed camouflage colors. Once it was draped over his weapon and his head, it would make him undetectable as it blended in with the forest behind him. Last of all, he brought out his suppressor that he screwed onto the end of the barrel.

He peered into the scope and made a minor adjustment to the bipod. On a whim, he decided to use the Frisbee he had brought along. If turned upside down, it could be used as a swivel base, giving greater mobility as he fired. After he sighted his first target, he used his range finder to accurately gauge the distance. Of course, he knew he had a variety of conditions to consider. Elevation: up thirty feet shooting downward. Humidity: high and a given in the hot-as-hell South. Wind velocity: dead calm. Temperature: close to ninety-five degrees. Light: mid-morning sun, above the tree line, offering a threat of a reflection from the scope lens. He'd used a honeycomb filter to deal with that. The rise of heat from the asphalt had managed to distort the view somewhat with wavy vapors. After doping the gun in consideration of all factors, he was chomping at the bit to take his first shot.

Once he had a bead on a black male, he placed his finger on the trigger, ready to take the shot. He had to make sure the selected target was stationary. Any movement could be a fuck-up, not lethal. The middle-aged man sat in a lawn chair, his head turned slightly to the right to better watch the musicians on stage. Although Jared was three hundred yards away, he could still hear the loud music through the massive speakers on either side of the stage. Jared considered how the cacophony created by electric guitars, drums, and keyboard could wreak havoc on a shooter's concentration, but not his. He had experienced accurate kill shots in worse chaos with deafening explosions from IEDs, grenade launchers, assault weapons, and surface-to-air missiles.

To Jared's disgust, the lead singer of the band got the girl groupies worked up when he hip-hopped his way to the edge of the stage to accept their outstretched hands. From what he had read online, it was a family-friendly band with squeaky-clean lyrics appropriate for the morning crowd. The rockers were scheduled to appear later.

Jared's first HVT (high value target), the black man, tapped his hands on the arms of his lawn chair, caught up in the music and oblivious to the people walking in front of the stage, the kids with balloons in the shapes of critters, the vendors selling hot dogs, hamburgers, and ice cream. *It's going to be easy, so easy,* Jared thought. He pulled the trigger.

The suppressor made the shot more like a whoosh than a blast. Jared watched the man's head jerk back from the impact, the top blown off, spouting a red mist. His flimsy chair fell over backwards. There was no time to watch the reaction of the people around him. He chambered the next bullet, found his target, and fired. The bullet went into the chest of another man, dark, but not African-American. Maybe Indian or Muslim. Definitely not American, he surmised.

Ten seconds for the next shot. *Damn! A near miss.* Bullet went into an old man's leg.

Focus, Bolten. Focus. Remember, they taught you to be a killing machine.

The band, unaware of what was happening, kept playing. The people close to the stage were just as clueless. Then everything changed. Someone screamed, drawing attention. Jared wondered if they had shouted a warning or blurted out the word *gun*. He was too far away to be sure.

What he did know was there was total bedlam in the park with people scrambling away, tripping over each other. Lawn chairs were knocked over, abandoned. Parents grabbed their children, carrying them as they ran. The massive speakers on each side of the stage knocked over. People tangled up in the cables that snaked across the grass to the sound system staging area.

A logjam at the entrance to the parking lot. Easy targets. No need to be selective. *Whoosh!* Another head shot. Total pandemonium. People knocking others down, out of the way. Children crying. Personal belongings abandoned on the ground.

Jared stayed composed, took his time so that the shots fired would be more effective, more lethal. With barely a blink of an eye, he engaged the bolt action that chambered the next bullet and fired. *Whoosh!* Target Number Four dropped. Blood gushed from her chest. Hispanic, he thought, because of her dark skin and raven hair. Young and pretty. Another shot. This time a woman, obese and slow moving. Bullet entered and exited her flabby arm, tearing flesh.

The next shot hit a tall man in the chest, went through him, and ended up in the groin area of the woman standing behind him. Blood gushed profusely from her leg. Jared figured the bullet hit her femoral artery. *You scared shitless bitch, hiding behind your man. Damn if that didn't cost you your life. You're gonna bleed out, honey, and soon!*

Jared saw that police moved in from all directions, but held their positions, seeking cover behind the open doors of their vehicles as they seemed to shout commands at the crowd, steering them to safety. EMS was on standby, too, he noticed, unable to offer any medical attention under constant fire.

In three minutes' time, Jared figured he had gotten off sixty shots, maybe more. He figured any minute SWAT would show up in their tripped-out vans or overpriced Bearcat, armored to the gills in protective gear. *Those fucking hotshots live and train for the day they can put their skills to use. I actually did them a favor.*

He brought the gun down, unscrewed the suppressor, and placed it in its case. Then, he folded up the drop cloth, making sure all the spent shells were on it, none left for the officers to send back to the lab. He tossed it into the rucksack and threw all his equipment over his shoulder. He had climbed up via an interior staircase, but he wanted his exit to be more dramatic. After he tucked his sidearm into the front of his pants, he flung the rappelling line to the ground and took a flying leap. He landed solid on his feet and took off in a run. Now his heart pounded, his head throbbed, and sweat leaked from every pore of his body. In a full sprint, he heard shouts, "Stop! Police! Show me your hands! Now!"

For only a second or two he froze, reached for his Glock that was now tucked in his front waistband, and spun around. The uniformed officer had his weapon out, but Jared fired first. The officer, young and a rookie, he assumed, fell to his knees, spurting blood from his thigh. *Damn shame. All that training gone to waste,* Jared thought.

As he made a mad dash to his vehicle, he heard the wail of sirens. Police, fire, medics. Far enough away, he no longer heard the screams of the crowd. Parked in a deserted stretch of a narrow side street surrounded by trees and brush, he didn't worry that anyone would see him. But he hadn't figured on a kid, a gangling boy of about twelve with a dazed look, his mouth hung open. The boy froze as he straddled his bike. *Maybe too stupid to be scared,* Jared thought. Of no threat; therefore, he wouldn't shoot him. He didn't kill children. Not on purpose, anyway. Besides, he wasn't worried about witnesses. He *wanted* folks to know he was responsible. His name would be legend. *Hell, they might write a song about me. A folk hero who had the courage to speak out.*

He knew he would be labeled as an active shooter, a direct threat, so what happened in the park was FPCON DELTA, a military code used to indicate an attack was happening. He felt a rush just thinking about it.

Before he took off in his truck, he wiped off the green, brown, and black gunk from his face. He switched to the cowboy hat, put on sunglasses, and then gunned the engine, leaving black tire marks on the asphalt. He laughed when he met two patrol cars speeding toward the park with their blue lights flashing and their sirens wailing. Like the other drivers, he pulled to the side of the road to stay out of their way. In his rearview mirror, he watched as they flew by in the opposite direction, unaware that the shooter was right before them. He chuckled as he gave them a little bye-bye wave.

§

Why was Independence Day celebrated in the hottest month of the year? Homicide Detective Chris Lagoni grumbled to himself. He tugged on his shirt collar and loosened his tie, wishing he had opted for casual wear. The more he mulled over the unbearable heat, the more he wondered why he and his partner, Nick Pulaski, had shown up at all. Today would be quiet, he hoped.

"Don't killers take the day off like everyone else?" he mumbled more to himself than to Nick and added, "Cook burgers and hot dogs on the grill, shoot fireworks, drink beer, get stoned, shoot-up. Well, there you go. They get wasted, get punchy, and want to shoot someone. Happens all the time. Their style of fireworks is the muzzle flash of a handgun."

"Lagoni, quit your bitching," Nick said. "We're here watching the pool hall for our number one suspect, so just chill out."

Chris gave a short sardonic laugh. "Chill out? Hell, I wish I could. It's gotta be...what? A hundred and twenty degrees in this damn car."

"Weather girl said a high of ninety-six today, but you're right. It's hotter than hell in here. I'll crank up the engine and turn on the A/C for a bit. Will that make you happy?"

"Yeah. Sure. You know something—I think my C.I. was jerking my chain. The dude's not coming. How 'bout we go across the street and get a Slurpee at the 7-Eleven?"

"Okay. My turn to buy. Then we'll head back to the station and make some calls. Maybe we can catch Lil' Mo and he'll agree to come in this time."

"In your dreams, Pulaski. He's out of state by now."

Fifteen minutes later, Chris watched Nick walk back to the car with a red Slurpee in each hand. With the engine running and the A/C cranked up, Chris hit the button to lower the driver's side window. He yelled, "Get in! Get in! Gotta roll. Active shooter at Montgomery Park. Massive casualties."

Nick stepped up his pace. He set the two jumbo cups on the sidewalk with their plastic red spoons planted vertically in the frozen mound like a flag.

"Damn! And I thought today would be a snoozer," Nick said as he flipped the switch for the flashing lights and siren.

CHAPTER TWO

By the time Chris and Nick were on scene, emergency personnel were like hornets swarming around a nest. There were so many first responders the detectives had trouble finding a place to park.

"Get that damn thing out of the way," a policeman in an orange vest shouted as Chris and Nick came to a stop parallel to the park. "Gotta keep this open for EMS. You gotta go back. Park in the next block."

Even showing their badges didn't help, so Chris whipped the car around and parked in front of someone's driveway. "What the heck," he muttered as he walked away.

When they arrived at the park and saw the carnage, Chris and Nick looked at each other in shock.

"Damn, this is a battleground. What kind of monster could do this?"

Nick nodded in agreement. "Uh-oh, the news media has shown up," he said, hitching his chin in the direction of a street not yet closed off. "Vultures, every damn one of them. It's going to be a circus."

A patrol cop, Officer Bates, walked up to them. They knew him well from times they had shown up at a crime scene and found that Bates, as a first responder, had secured the area in advance of their arrival. They liked him for his professionalism in dealing with onlookers and family members. It made their jobs easier to perform.

From the temperature and excitement, Bates wiped sweat from his forehead with the bend of his arm and said, "You guys better report in to Captain Webb. I've been told he heads up the ALERT team—the tall dude with the spikey red hair standing in front of that big-ass mobile unit." They looked over to where Bates pointed and saw Webb standing in front of the command center. Bates pulled out a handkerchief from his pocket to dab at newly-formed beads of sweat. He added, "And just to give you a heads-up, Special Agent Calhoun was asking about you homicide guys. Said to tell you boys to report in to him after you check in with Webb."

"Sure. We understand protocol, don't we, Nick?"

Nick gave a sardonic grin similar to the one Chris gave the officer. "Yeah. Sure. This is the FBI's show. We get that."

As they walked away from Bates, Chris muttered, "Calhoun can go fuck himself. And the rest of those feds can, too. Bunch of pricks."

"Still pissed at 'em, huh?"

"Past history," Chris snapped.

"Yeah, sure."

Chris let Nick's remark go unchallenged.

Before they reported to anyone they took a minute to survey the horrific scene. They understood that their role would be as part of a team to preserve the crime scene and investigate, while others would be charged with getting the injured to the trauma area where they were treated on the scene before being transported to one of the area hospitals. It was a balancing act with one team not jeopardizing the work of the other.

People stood around in clusters, the horror of the scene written on their faces. Some looked dazed and lethargic as if not attuned to the reality of what had happened. With little success, deputies urged anyone not helping to leave the area. Being somewhat compliant, they moved behind the yellow tape.

When the detectives checked in with Captain Webb, he did nothing more than add their names to a log and tell them to find where they were needed. Walking back toward the crime scene, the detectives saw a tall bald guy making his way toward them. His wraparound Oakley sunglasses augmented his standing as tough guy and former military brass. Broad shoulders and large biceps indicated serious muscle under his starched dress shirt. His photo ID tag dangled from around his neck like a warning label that seemed to say, *don't mess with me.*

Despite Chris's mixed feelings for the man, he greeted FBI Special Agent Hank Calhoun with a hearty handshake.

"You guys know the drill," Calhoun said. "We'll let you know what we need. We've got a net around the city. He drove off in a vehicle he had parked at a distance. Got highway patrol, state police on the lookout. Of course, any other form of transport out of the city."

"Got a description?" Nick asked.

"Some kid saw a guy wearing camo with his face painted up to match, running towards the woods with a rifle and a sack. Other than giving us that, the kid wasn't much help. Too scared, I guess. He didn't see his getaway vehicle, but we found fresh tire marks on the road. I've got a team going door to door near where we think he parked."

"Where do you want us?" Chris asked.

Calhoun looked out at the scene and rubbed his jaw. His gaze bounced back and forth from Nick to Chris. "Tell you what, you guys find people taking videos with their cell phones or cameras. We'll need to do a scene reenactment. Call me on the radio if you get anything I need to know about."

He walked away abruptly, ending any further discussion. Chris looked at Nick and frowned. "Busy work."

"I know what you want to do—go catch the son of a bitch."

"Damn right. Okay, let's go do what the man said. Video. Maybe there's a surveillance camera somewhere. Let's talk to those guys on the stage."

A crew of stagehands were packing up sound equipment since all scheduled events of the day had been cancelled. They worked at a frantic pace, obviously still shaken. A section of the decorative red, white, and blue backdrop had been torn by fleeing spectators. The ripped blue field with white stars was forever separated from its red and white stripes, hanging precariously and flapping in the gentle breeze. Props, microphones and a set of drums rested haphazardly on their sides, knocked over during the ensuing stampede to escape the mêlée.

The detectives approached a skinny guy in a Yankees ball cap wrapping a coil of cable around his arm. As Chris held out his police badge, he said, "Excuse me. We need to know if the concert was videotaped. If you panned out over the crowd during the shooting."

Skinny guy shrugged his shoulders. "You need to talk to the band manager about that."

"Okay. Where can I find him?"

"He left with the band. They cut out of here real quick. You know—security issues. In case the band was targeted."

"Yeah, well, who else around here might know something?"

"That lady behind the stage might know. She's in charge. All the organizers are back there. They had a big spread set up. Their own private party."

"Thanks. We'll see if we can find her."

On their way, Nick and Chris heard someone crying, and frantic voices let them know that something was as bad behind the stage as the scene in front. The detectives exchanged questioning looks and hurried back there.

A group of people, two women and three men, formed a circle as they talked with police officers. One of the men had his hands on a shoulder of each woman, offering comfort. When Chris and Nick approached them, one of the women stopped bawling and looked their way.

The two officers took the detectives aside. The tall one said, "There's a subject behind the bushes over there. Near the brick wall. Deceased. Gunshot."

"From the shooter?" Nick asked. "How can that be? I thought he only fired into the crowd in front of the stage.

Unless the victim ran back here after getting shot."

Both officers shook their heads. The more senior of the two said, "This guy was shot with a handgun, not a rifle—a .38. See the blood spatter?" he said, pointing toward the low brick wall that separated the park from the parking lot. Next he held up a sealed plastic bag for their inspection. It held the bullet. "We got lucky. The guy took a hit to the chest—went clean through him and into the wall."

Chris ran his hand down his face. "Damn. Any witnesses?"

"You need to talk to the ladies. Listen, guys, the victim is a big deal—make that was a big deal. He was the guest of honor. A retired army colonel. Got the Bronze Star, Silver Star, and a Purple Heart. He was a commander in Nam."

"Thanks for the heads up. C'mon, Nick, let's go talk to the ladies."

There was an exchange of introductions where the detectives learned that the ladies, both in their fifties with similar dark hair with streaks of gray, were co-chairpersons of the committee that organized the day's events. Julie Thompson and Betty Ramsey were still shaken, as evidenced by their tear-stained cheeks. Chris turned to the one that seemed the more composed of the two.

"Mrs. Thompson, I know this is hard, but can you tell us what you saw?"

He got more than he bargained for. She sucked in a jagged breath and said, "Colonel Mahoney was our keynote speaker. He was to speak after lunch right after members of the military and their families were to be honored. Then the National Guard Drill Team was set to perform. Thank God the high school students hadn't arrived yet. They were scheduled to sing the national anthem and a few patriotic songs. Can you imagine those kids having to experience this tragedy? Everything is ruined! All our planning, and the poor colonel...a nice man. He flew in from Palm Springs just this morning. What a tragedy.

You'll catch the man who did this, won't you?"

Frustrated by her redirection of his question, he turned to Nick to respond to her plea. "Ma'am, we're going to do our best," he said. "We really need you to tell us what you saw."

With a tissue pressed against her cheek, Julie talked through fresh tears. "I saw Colonel Mahoney talking off to the side with some man. They kept moving farther away from us, so that I couldn't hear a thing they were saying. They seemed to be in an argument. Then we heard screams out front, and we all ran over near the stage to see what was happening. The colonel must have stayed back with the man. Then we found him lying against the bush and no sign of the other man."

She covered her face with her hands and sobbed.

"Can you tell us about the man, Mrs. Thompson?" Chris asked."Did you get a good look?"

She looked over at her co-chair. "Betty, what would you say? Maybe in his thirties? Big guy. Tall. Athletic. Sandy hair, cut short. He wore cargo pants and a dark green T-shirt."

"I think his shirt was navy, Julie. It looked to me like his hair was darker, maybe black. I pegged the guy to be around forty, not thirty. But you're right. He did look physically fit."

Chris felt more frustration in the inconsistency of their descriptions, but he kept his thoughts to himself. From his experience, he found that witnesses were never that accurate and sometimes multiple witnesses were all over the map.

Nick asked, "Anything different about this guy? I mean, anything that might set him apart?"

The ladies looked at each other and nodded. Finally, Julie said, "Omigosh. We forgot to tell you the most important part. The man had only one arm. His left arm was gone. No prosthetic either."

Now we're getting somewhere.

"Thanks, ladies. You've been a big help." Chris looked at his partner. "Let's go take a look at the victim."

The colonel was dressed in a business suit, minus the jacket. Lying on his back, they could see he had taken a hit to the chest, where blood coated his shirt front. His tie was flipped up over his shoulder. Mahoney was a tall figure with broad shoulders, but his military physique had gone to pot, especially around his middle.

Chris put his hands on his knees and stood up from a squat. "Well, we better let Calhoun know."

Only five minutes after Nick radioed the FBI agent, he showed up. Abruptly bending over the victim, his ID tag swung forward from the chain around his neck. With his mouth closed, his tongue oddly moved around in circles and puffed out one cheek like a plug of tobacco. As if in deep thought, he silently studied the body and then grunted. With thumbs hooked over his belt, he stood up straight and said, "Guess we're looking at two shooters. Better get the word out. I'll tell the team to see if any of the other victims were shot with a .38."

"That doesn't make sense," Chris said. "The shooter wouldn't put himself out there knowing someone else was shooting everything in sight with a high-powered rifle."

"He might have known the sniper wasn't shooting close to the stage, just further back. They worked out a plan in advance."

"I don't see it, sir."

"Lagoni, two shooters working together. That's what we've got, so deal with it. You guys investigate this for now until I can get a team over here."

"What about the video you asked us to get?" Nick asked.

"Forget that. Stay with this until I get a team over here."

Nick stared as if his pupils projected an imaginary laser pointer on Calhoun's back as he walked away. Chris tapped him on the arm. "What he's really saying is stay out of his hair."

"He doesn't have any."

"Then it shouldn't be too hard, Pulaski."

§

Chris said an emphatic *no* to Nick's agreeable nod to the deputies standing over the body of Colonel Gerald Mahoney.

"Chris, we gotta let them take the body," Nick said. "They've set up a temporary morgue over there. The M.E. has already been here and released the body. So let these guys do their job and take it."

"I said NO! This is an active crime scene. Separate from the other. This is CMPD's case, not the fucking FBI's. Not related to their shooter."

"We don't know that! C'mon, Chris, don't be a hard-ass. Remember what happened the last time you got into it with the feds?"

"Our crime scene investigators are on their way. Be here in ten minutes. We wait."

The deputies that surrounded the body and prepared to bag it and cart it away looked like they could out-muscle the two of them, but that did not deter Chris. He held firm. They muttered curses under their breath, but backed away.

Their leader said, "Okay, detective. Whatever. It's not like we don't have other things to do. We'll be back."

Almost as soon as the deputies walked away, Chris heard his name called. He turned to see a patrol officer everyone called Stinger waving his arm to get his attention. He stood near a stand of bushes that ran parallel to the sidewalk. When Chris and Nick hustled over to see what he had, he pointed to a cell phone laying in the dirt underneath a bush.

Chris slipped on Latex gloves and picked it up. "What do we have here? Could have been dropped by someone running away, or maybe the killer dropped it. Feeling lucky, Pulaski?"

Stinger said, "The hot dog vendor said he saw a man run by this way after the shooting started. A one-armed guy. Big dude."

"Interesting."

Chris inspected the cell phone almost with envy because it was a newer model of his own with added features. He clicked on Gallery, hoping they might find a photo of the cell owner. They found a few shots taken of a woman, young and pretty with a dazzling smile for the camera. One pose of her had a man at her side, a tall solid man, also smiling. He had one arm around her shoulder; his other arm was missing.

"Hell yeah!" Chris gave a triumphant holler. "This is our guy."

Just as he started to click on the contacts button, the phone rang. A photo and name appeared on the display. Chris recognized her as the same woman in the photos. He swiped his finger across the glass to take the call and put it on speaker for Nick's benefit.

"Hi, Sammy, it's me," the voice said. "My plane just landed. Look, I know you're upset, but you need to calm down. We'll stick to the original plan—just like we talked about. It's going to be okay. Just trust me. Look, it might be a while before I can get off—I'm in the back, and of course everyone is getting carry-on luggage from the overhead compartment. Then I have to stop by the restroom. Just go to the cell lot and I'll call you. You can pick me up outside baggage claim. Okay?"

"Sure. See ya," Chris answered in a voice not his.

Nick laughed as he watched Chris push the end-call button. "What's with the phony deep voice? You sounded like you've been eating gravel."

"Did you hear that? We gotta roll, Nick. This is it. This is the girlfriend of the shooter. Gotta be. Did you hear what she said— 'Stick to the original plan?' We got her name and photo from the phone display. Megan Moore. Let's go pick her up from the airport. Shouldn't keep the lady waiting."

"We should tell someone where we're going."

"Hell no."

"But Calhoun—Captain Bowers. Our own damn boss. At least tell Holden. We can't just go—"

"No time. We pick her up and she tells us who this guy is."

"Oh, sure. Piece of cake," Nick said.

"Did you see her photo? Now how much trouble can a girl that looks that sweet give us?"

CHAPTER THREE

N ot until they reached the sign for arriving flights at Charlotte Douglas International Airport did Nick turned off the flashing lights to the unmarked sedan. With his elbow resting on the window opening and his fingers nervously tapping the door frame, Chris cursed when the line of cars slowed to a crawl. They were forced to stop at a crosswalk while passengers walked in front of two lanes of stopped vehicles, wheeling their luggage behind them. With squinted eyes, Chris strained to pick out the lady he had seen on the cell phone display.

Although he had only a brief glance before he answered the call, her image was etched in his memory. He couldn't forget the striking brunette with a sexy smile and alluring green eyes. In his opinion, she looked to be in her twenties, thirty at the most, but certainly young and beautiful. He wondered how a killer could score such a catch.

"Megan Moore, where are you, sweetie? Come on, come on. Come to Daddy."

Nick laughed. "You probably scared her away with your creepy voice."

Again Chris had used the exaggerated deep voice when she called to say she just got her luggage and would be right outside Door B.

"Nope! There she is," Chris exclaimed. "Pull over, Nick."

If Chris could order up a dream girl, this woman would be it. Looking out at the line of cars curbside, she ran her hand through tresses of chestnut hair and pursed her luscious lips as if impatient with the delay.

Nick said, "Holy shit! She's even prettier in person. Our friend Sammy is one lucky dude."

As soon as Nick stopped the car, Chris hopped out. He flashed his badge for her to see. She glanced at it as though he had shown her a dead rat. A dislike of law enforcement or authority, Chris assumed.

"Are you Megan Moore?"

"Why do you ask?"

Despite her dismissive attitude, he stepped closer, picking up the scent of her perfume and staring down into seductive green eyes. He cleared his throat before he spoke. "Miss Moore, I'm Detective Chris Lagoni with Charlotte-Mecklenburg Police. And behind the wheel is Detective Nick Pulaski. We'd like you to come with us, please."

"I didn't witness the scuffle in baggage claim, so I can't help you. Now if you'll excuse me, I'm waiting for someone to pick me up."

She gave a yank on the handle of her luggage so that it tilted back on its wheels. She stepped around him and proceeded to roll the case behind her. Chris put a hand on her arm that made her come to an abrupt halt.

"Your ride is not coming," he said in a somber voice. "This has nothing to do with whatever happened in baggage claim. You need to come with us."

She stared at him as if trying to make sense of his words. He wondered if he needed to repeat it, but then she said, "What's going on? Where is Sam?"

Chris held up the cell phone for her to see. "Is this his cell?"

She refused to answer, so he said, "Miss Moore, this is the phone you just called and asked Sam to pick you up. You were speaking to me."

Her face turned ashen. Because she looked like she might reel backwards, he gripped her arm to keep her upright. There was panic in her voice when she said, "Where's Sam? Why do you have his phone?"

"We'll tell you everything when you come with us."

But she stayed stationary when he tried to escort her away. She curled her lips in a pout. *Spoiled, high-maintenance woman.* The thought crossed Chris's mind, but he didn't want to jump to any conclusion. Besides, he felt she had a right to be distrustful. What gave them the authority to show up, tell her nothing, and then expect her to ride away with them?

"Is Sam hurt?" she asked.

"No, nothing like that."

"Then what? If you want me to get in that car, then you better tell me *something.*"

Chris stared down at the asphalt and let out an exasperated breath. "Your friend Sam might be in danger. We need your cooperation so we can help him."

A lie that worked. She covered her mouth with both hands. "Oh, my God! Sammy? Oh, no! Okay, okay. I'll go with you, but you better tell me what's going on."

"We will when we get there."

Chris held the rear door open for her. In a gesture to coax her inside, his hand extended precariously close to her waistline but did not make contact. After she was seated inside the car, he closed the door and placed her luggage in the trunk.

Behind the wheel, Nick glanced at Chris, who had just settled into the front passenger seat. "Where to? The command center on site?"

"No. Downtown. This is our investigation for now. Don't need Calhoun to muck it up."

"Okay," Nick said with a shrug. "It's your funeral."

Once they turned on Billy Graham Parkway heading away from the airport, the police scanner crackled. Chris turned the volume down to keep the woman in the back seat from knowing what was going on. They'd hit her cold, clueless, and take advantage of what they knew and she didn't. *Know the answer before you ask the question* was an interrogation technique Chris learned from six years in homicide.

"Did you catch that, Chris?" Nick said, straining to hear the voice coming through the radio.

"Nah, but something's going on."

Just then, Chris's cell phone rang. He listened intently to the caller feeding him new information from the crime scene. With a shocked look, he locked eyes with Nick. Once his call ended, he slammed his fist onto the dashboard and ordered Nick to pull over.

Nick maneuvered the car to the side of the road. "What—what? Just tell me, Lagoni. What the hell?"

"Stop the damn car. Get out, and I'll tell you. Not in front of—" He gestured at the back seat, and Nick nodded with understanding.

Outside the car, Chris showed signs of anger that made Nick keep his distance. He felt like cursing, punching something, hell, maybe even shooting something or somebody. He was pissed, and he wanted Nick and the woman in the car to know it.

"The guy in the tower—he killed one of ours!" he told Nick. "A rookie on the job six months. Our guy confronted the shooter as he was fleeing. He took a hit to the leg. Bled out. Just a damn kid, Nick! A damn kid!"

"Shit!"

"This is war!" Chris said. "I don't give a shit what Calhoun says. This is *our* fight. One of our guys."

"Okay, Chris. We'll get him. First, we'll get the name of this other shooter, this 'Sammy', and see if he's tied in with the sniper, and we'll go from there. Let's take the woman in and see what she can tell us."

"If she's in on this, I'll rip her throat out."

Nick placed his hand on Chris's arm. "We won't get anywhere if you go ballistic. So cool it, Chris."

Back in the car and again on the road, silence seemed to magnify the intensity inside the car. Chris was relieved that the woman stayed silent and did not ask about his fit of anger that he was sure she had witnessed. Nick pulled in to the underground bay at police headquarters. As Chris assisted the woman out, he noted that her demeanor had changed since they had picked her up. Whatever was going on inside her head, she kept her thoughts to herself.

"Come with us," Nick said to her.

When they exited the elevator on the floor with signs marked Criminal Investigations, her body stiffened. With a petulant look directed first at Nick and then Chris, she stayed silent and allowed them to lead the way down the corridor.

§

She hesitated when Nick asked for the full name and address of Sam, the man she had called.

"Answer him," Chris said. "We wouldn't ask if it wasn't important." Her refusal to respond challenged Chris's patience. With a hard stare, he added, "Did you note the sign coming in? This is not the Missing Persons Division."

"You lied to me. Sam isn't in any danger, is he?"

"He could be, but we'll get to that. We're with Homicide. Don't hinder our investigation, Miss Moore. Please don't do that."

She licked her lips and rolled her shoulders back. "His full name is Samuel Benjamin Briggs. His address is 1504 Vandy Drive. Now your turn, detective, tell me what is going on."

Nick looked at Chris. They had been partners long enough to read each other's mind. Chris figured Nick was trying to say, *Is she going to play dumb?*

Chris said, "Miss Moore, on the phone call to Sam you said, 'Let's stick to the plan.' What was the plan?"

She didn't answer. Megan Moore, a distraction in a pink sundress that inched up to mid-thigh, bit down on her luscious lower lip. Wherever she had been before she flew into Charlotte, she had received a nice tan. *Maybe spent a few days on the beach as she and the Sam guy planned mass murder,*

Chris thought. She stared and blinked several times at Chris as though she was going to wait him out.

With a defiant tilt of the chin, she said, "Detective, I'm not answering any of your questions until you answer mine. Where is Sam? What has happened?"

"You want to know what has happened," Chris said, leaning back in his seat and hooking his thumbs over his belt. "Okay, I'll tell you, Miss Moore. There was an active shooter at Montgomery Park. There are multiple casualties. Sam was involved. He killed at least one person, maybe more."

"You're lying. He would never do that!"

"A witness saw him." That was a stretch, but he'd make her believe it anyway. "Sam Briggs dropped his cell phone as he ran. The phone I showed you." Chris paused to let her digest the information, then said, "Back to my question. What was the plan? To kill an unarmed, innocent man?"

"This is all a big mistake. Someone must have stolen Sam's phone. It couldn't have been Sam because he would never have gone to that park, especially on a day that they're having a big Fourth of July celebration. Impossible."

"Why do you say that?" Nick asked, his brow raised with intrigue.

"He avoids crowds. The noise, the people, the smells, the traffic. I know—I was with him at a free concert downtown and he freaked out, couldn't handle it. The war did that to him."

"Like I said," Chris said, "we have an eyewitness of a one-armed man running away right after the shooting. He dropped this phone. That's a fact. For the third time, I'll ask you—what was the plan mentioned in your message?"

"*The plan* was to see a lawyer."

"About what?"

"Legal advice."

Chris sucked in his lower lip and stared at her. He found that her eyes had softened as if the severity of their interrogation had suddenly hit her. She sat very still, one leg crossed over the other, looking as sweet and innocent as a kitten yawning from its nap. But he wouldn't let her vulnerability affect his job. He wasn't a patient man, and he wanted answers. On better days, he would have found a more genteel approach to demanding answers to pertinent questions.

"Sam Briggs seeks legal advice in advance of killing someone? That's planning ahead. Impressive!" Chris thought he heard Nick groan in protest to his absurd remark. Unaffected by his partner's caveat or Megan's stare, he proceeded by asking, "Please explain, Miss Moore. Legal advice?"

"He—I mean Sam, just got a letter that denied his workers' comp claim. I told him if it got denied, our next step was to get some legal advice."

Chris locked eyes with Nick, but this time he couldn't read his thoughts. Chris directed his gaze back at her. "Miss Moore, what is your relationship with this man?"

"We're friends."

"Just friends? Nothing more?"

"Neighbors, actually."

After a machine-gun battery of questions, she provided no answers of any use. Repeatedly, she denied any knowledge or involvement. The time came when she gave both men only a hard stare rather than a response.

Unfazed, Chris pushed his chair back and stood up. He waited for Nick to do the same and then said, "We'll be back, Miss Moore. Want anything? Water? Soda?"

"I want to go home."

As soon as they stepped outside the interview room, Nick said, "We call it in. Tell Calhoun we ID'd the second shooter. Guess we better get Sergeant Holden on board with this, too."

"Yeah, you're right. We'll do it by the book, at least until my gut tells me differently."

Chris felt Nick's stare and when their eyes met, Nick said,

"What's eating you, Chris?"

"Nothing," he said with a dismissive shrug.

"Something is. What is it?"

"I wish she wasn't so damn pretty."

CHAPTER FOUR

"Good work," Calhoun said over the phone. The comment took Chris by surprise since it was the first time the agent had ever said anything close to a compliment. The two men rarely crossed paths, and as far as Chris was concerned, that was a good thing.

"Now we have a positive ID for both shooters," Calhoun said. "The sniper left a flash drive in the tower with a letter to America and signed his whole freaking name. Jared Henry Bolten. He wants to be famous. We'll grant him his wish in federal court as soon as we catch the bastard and put shackles on him.

"I'll email the document to you, Lagoni. See what you think— if your guy is the same nut job as the sniper. We'll find a link, just a matter of time. Get started on a warrant. Rush job. As soon as you've got it, I'll get my team together and we'll meet you at his residence. Now who's this woman you picked up?"

"Her name is Megan Moore. I'm not sure if she's in the middle of this or not. She's not exactly forthcoming."

"Keep at her," Calhoun said. "Sending the doc as soon as we hang up."

§

Thirty miles outside of the city and in his daddy's pickup, Jared stopped at a minute market for a six-pack of Red Bull and AA and D batteries. He needed a shot of energy the drink would provide him and also energy for battery-powered items in his underground bunker. He didn't know how long he'd have to stay there until he could surface and make his getaway to Mexico. Right now, the feds would be looking for the shooter to leave the country. All airports, bus terminals, and train stations would be watched.

He figured his mug shot was being sent to every law enforcement agency and shown on television networks across the country, hell, maybe the world. Unless a person was on another planet, his name would be on their lips and his image etched into their brains. He didn't know of any other shooter who had accomplished what he had. The fatality count was high. He'd left behind a trail of carnage never seen before and on the nation's freaking birthday. But it was *his* independence that was declared on the Fourth of July.

If he could, he'd give a one-finger salute to every fucking politician in the country. He said as much in his manifesto that was probably going viral by now. All a person had to do was Google his name, and it would take them right to his website. He liked the photo of himself on the homepage. A serious warrior in his Army dress uniform complete with the medals and ribbons he'd earned in battle. Of course, holding his Remington 700 rifle added a special touch. When he had walked off base and was declared AWOL, he had thought of burning everything he possessed that was associated with the US Army, including his uniform, but he was glad he'd saved all that shit for the photograph. He boasted about his ability to capture the dignified pose of himself with the help of the timer on his camera. His website looked professional, complete with videos of himself in action, blowing up things with homemade bombs, bull's-eye shots at targets with his rifle from a distance of 200 yards, and still shots of a plywood cutout shot to hell with his AK-47.

A sheriff's deputy entered the Minute Market and walked over to the same refrigerated case where Jared stood. He heard the deputy's radio crackle. The officer's utility belt squeaked under the weight of all the tools of his trade including a .40 caliber handgun and Taser. It was clear to Jared that the guy was jacked up, almost certainly about the shooting, which made him laugh inwardly. The poor guy had no idea he was standing next to the shooter. Jared had gone to great lengths to disguise his looks so that he didn't look like the same person from his Facebook page and website photos and even different from his mug shot. His hair was now dyed dark brown and grown out so that it hung scraggily around his collar. He sported a full beard and was pleased that it matched perfectly with his new hair color. He wore his black cowboy hat tilted forward so that it covered most of his forehead. The lens of his aviator sunglasses were so dark no one could make out his eyes. No sirree, he did not look anything like his circulated mug shot.

"You seem to be in a hurry, officer. Has something happened I should know about?" he said with a concerned look.

"There was a massive shooting at a park in Charlotte. The shooter is on the loose. We've got a BOLO out for him. The fella could be headed our way."

"Good God! That's awful! Hope you catch the bastard."

"Oh, we will, we will. Just a matter of time."

After the clerk waved him off as he tried to pay for bottled water, the deputy scurried back to his official vehicle and tore out of the parking lot. Jared couldn't let his joy show. For the sake of the cashier, he faked a solemn look and paid in cash for his merchandise.

§

It had been close to five hours since Bolten's reign of terror had ended and he'd made his getaway. In that time, they had learned his name, address, criminal record, and registered vehicle. His Ford 150 pickup had been found parked at his home. The engine was cold and a neighbor said it had been there all day. Using a battering ram, the SWAT team got inside the shabby two-bedroom house that he rented. There was no sign of Bolten, although a poster propped up on a kitchen chair had a message for them: *Can't Catch Me. Go Fuck Yourselves.* As if adding further insult, he had used his artistic talent to draw a hand making a one-finger salute.

Officers paid a visit to his mother's residence a mile away down a winding two-lane road. Mrs. Bolten seemed confused and upset that agents, suited-up as if to do battle, showed up on her front porch. It was obvious to them that she had no knowledge of her son's activities. She offered one valuable clue. Her deceased husband's pickup was missing.

"Sometimes my boy comes over to use it," she told them. "He keeps it running and in good shape. I figured he took it this morning before I got out of bed. Didn't think anything about it, really. He comes and goes as he pleases. I gave up on that boy long ago." She paused as if what the agents had told her about her son's actions suddenly sank in. "Now, tell me again. You think my boy is responsible for a shooting at a park where a lot of people got hurt or killed? Oh, Lord," she muttered, covering her lips with her fingertips. "Please tell me it ain't so."

Immediately the word went out to all agencies and to the media that authorities were now searching for a medium blue Dodge Ram pickup with an empty gun rack and a dent in the left front fender. Also, according to a neighbor, it was believed to have a Confederate flag sticker in the rear window.

"It should be easy to spot," Calhoun told his team of agents.

§

The mobile command center was too small to fit all the personnel inside. Special Agent Calhoun had gathered leadership from state police, CMPD, Mecklenburg County Sheriff's Office, FBI, and Homeland Security for an urgent meeting at three o'clock. Ironically, they met at the same church where the sniper had used the tower as a firing platform.

The Charlotte-Mecklenburg Police Department was well represented in Calhoun's hastily called meeting inside a Sunday school classroom. At a long folding table and seated in metal chairs were Sergeant Holden, Captain Bowers, and Major Lackey, all from CMPD's Criminal Investigation Department. While Special Agent Calhoun engaged in a casual conversation with Mecklenburg County Sheriff Carson, Chief of Police Steve Blackwell silently glared at them from across the room. The mood in the room was somber. Chatter lacked the usual bravado and one-upmanship associated with law enforcement. CMPD officers took it personally that one of their own had died at the hands of the killer, and they wanted answers, and they wanted them now.

As people were still finding places around the table, Chief Blackwell took Calhoun aside and got in his face. With hands on hips, he leaned forward as though to prevent the special agent's escape. Red-faced and with a clenched jaw, he said, "This guy was already on your watch list? Your agency let this guy slip through the cracks so he could go out and shoot anyone in his sights. You guys dropped the ball." After a pause to let Calhoun respond, the agent only stared back at him. "Say something, Calhoun! Tell me I've got it wrong. Please!"

Calhoun tilted his chin up and puffed his chest out in a defensive pose. "We didn't have enough to suspect he was a threat. Do you have any idea how many nut jobs we're supposed to be watching? Thousands! We can't have our eye on every damn one of them. Not possible."

Shaking his head in disgust, Chief Blackwell walked back to his seat. When everyone had settled into their places, Calhoun began the briefing. Like a military officer addressing fighter pilots before a dogfight, he stood at the head of the table with his hands behind his back. A large man with a shaved head and square jaw, he presented a commanding appearance, a trait rumored to be instrumental in his promotion to special agent of the Charlotte division.

"Here's what we know so far," he began. "Suspect is Jared Henry Bolten, age thirty-one, a resident of Gaston County, former military—Army—where he trained as a sniper, dishonorably discharged in 2010, and currently employed as a brick mason. He is known as a hothead, a loner, and has been in multiple scrapes with the law from traffic violations to public intoxication and assault. This morning he used a Remington 700 rifle with a suppressor and discharged approximately seventy to eighty rounds with a .308 cartridge, 168 match grade." Calhoun paused to exhale a long breath and run his hand over his bald head. He then continued. "As he made his getaway, Bolten was confronted by Officer Jeremy Hawkins, who he shot and killed with a handgun. Agents have been to Bolten's residence and found an empty storage locker where we believe he kept several rifles, handguns, explosives, and assault weapons. We discovered photos on his website of where he photographed these items, and we were able to match up the locations where they were present on the property. All have been removed." Calhoun nodded as a go-ahead to one of his team members. "Agent Drummond is passing out a photo of the suspect along with a physical description and details about the vehicle he is believed to be using. Also, for your entertainment is a copy of Bolten's letter to America that was on a flash drive he left in the bell tower for us to find. Keep in mind, this letter he wrote is *not* for release to the public. Classified, gentlemen."

Calhoun sat down while the officers read over the documents. Chief Blackwell made a sour face as he read what Bolten had written.

Independence Day, July 4, 2014

Dear America,

Have I gotten your attention yet? You forced me to take action that would spill blood, kill, maim, injure, and traumatize people. Young, old, strong, weak. I don't give a shit.

Your country, yes, the good old US of A has done the same all over the world. Remember Iwo Jima, Nagasaki, Vietnam, Korea, Iraq, Afghanistan, Pakistan? The government is proud of all the carnage. We are the bullies of the world. Don't ever doubt that.

I killed my share of ragheads and got a hard-on every time I pulled the trigger and nailed the motherfuckers. My job was to protect the infantry patrols in urban areas and in the desert. I'd get a bead on the enemy and get the green light to fire. Boom! One less asshole to deal with. But the government wants to punish me for doing my job. Can you believe it? That is fucking messed up!

Back home is where the real war is. Politicians lining their pockets, a liberal administration wanting to make this country a socialist nation, and the NSA spying on private citizens. I sure as hell don't want to work my ass off so my tax dollars can go for Medicaid, food stamps, and liberal causes. Those tree-hugging faggots can just fuck themselves and leave the rest of us the hell alone.

The army trained me well. I'm a fucking killing machine. That's why today there will be bodies everywhere. It's the only way to get my message across. Something needs to change. Read my postings on my website and educate yourself.

I despise the federal government and their iron rule. Before you know it, the feds will take away our guns. Guys like Rush Limbaugh have it right, but some people think they're crackpots. I don't. If you listen to what they're saying, you'll see that what they say makes sense.

Wake up, America! Revolt while there's still time.

Your comrade in arms,
Jared Henry Bolten

When all present had enough time to review the documents, Calhoun continued, "Now you see what we're dealing with. We've contacted the commanding officer at Fort Benning and he has confirmed that Bolten was with the 3rd Battalion, 75th Ranger Regiment and served multiple deployments to Iraq and Afghanistan. He is trained as an Army Ranger and sniper. He scored above average in testing and had the highest score as a marksman in his unit. While in Afghanistan, he was recommended for court martial after he beat up and almost killed another soldier—his spotter, who reported him for taking kill shots at unarmed civilians in Afghanistan. When he returned to the U.S., he walked off base rather than answer the charges against him. He was dishonorably discharged in 2010 and went to work as a brick mason until he quit two days ago.

"We believe Bolten teamed up with a man named Samuel Benjamin Briggs, also former military and served in Iraq and Afghanistan. So far we know he has killed Colonel Gerald Mahoney with a .38 revolver at about the same time as the other shootings. As yet, we have not found any other victims shot by this weapon, but all the victims' injuries have not been thoroughly reviewed. We are looking into how these two men knew each other. Probably served together overseas. Any questions about the suspects before I move on to the investigation?"

Chief Blackmon reared back in his chair and looked up at Calhoun. "Agent Calhoun," he said and paused intentionally, "it is my suggestion that you sit on the information about the second shooter until we know more. Otherwise you will have a media circus and panic throughout the city like you've never seen before. Let's get our facts straight before we go off the deep end about a second shooter."

The air didn't stir as all waited for the special agent's response. He put a laser beam stare on the police chief's forehead that would have been lethal had it been a weapon. "Thank you for your concerns, chief. I'll remind you that the FBI has the lead on the investigation, and I take my orders from the director himself, who has been briefed from the moment we got the call. Now, as I was saying, we'll discuss the search efforts for Bolten."

CHAPTER FIVE

As soon as the ink was dry on the signed search warrant, Chris and Nick headed over to the condominium owned by Sam Briggs. His registered vehicle, parked out front, made them and the feds suspicious that he was holed up inside. With no response to their knock, the FBI team gained entrance with a battering ram. Once each room was cleared, the group descended on the interior like flies on a picnic.

Megan had been left alone in the interview room for almost two hours when the detectives returned. They found her with her head resting on her arm. Her dark tresses covered her face and they wondered if she had fallen asleep. In her pink and white halter dress, her back was exposed, showing a horizontal tan line where her bikini top had prevented exposure to the sun. The hemline of her dress had crawled further up, giving them a nice view of her shapely legs. In Chris's mind, her casual attire, nice tan, and impromptu nap made her appear like an intoxicated young lady sitting at a beach bar. When he exchanged a look with Nick, his partner winked as if he could read his depraved mind.

When Nick closed the door, she came to life, sitting up straight and pushing her hair away from her face. She rubbed her eyes into wakefulness and said, "You're back."

"Yes, ma'am," Chris said. He tossed a manila file onto the table to stir a reaction from her. He noted her raised brow and knew he had piqued her interest. After he took a seat, he leaned forward and put one elbow up on the table as his hands comfortably folded one over the other. "Would you like to go home soon, Miss Moore?"

"Of course! I can't tell you where Sam is. Believe me, I want to find him as much as you do. I've been out of town. Visiting my family in Florida. I came back a day early because Sam was upset, but I haven't spoken to him since yesterday. I have no idea where he is or what he's up to. I'm actually very worried about him."

"You've been lying to us," Chris said.

Her eyes widened. "Why would I do that?"

"You were more than friends with Sam Briggs, so let's cut to the chase, Miss Moore. You and Briggs are lovers. We have proof."

Her expression was more incredulous than before. She seemed too stunned to speak, but then she found her voice. "No we're not! Never have been. We're friends. I told you!"

Without a word, Chris opened the file folder and set out a row of three items in front of her. He pointed at each one. "Look at these, Miss Moore. Photos of you we found in his condo. Not the type you give a friend. A lover, but not a friend."

With one hand covering her lips, she leaned forward to examine each one and then closed her eyes. Even viewing them upside down, Chris found the photos provocative. In one, she wore a bikini as she stretched out on a beach towel. In another, she leaned forward so that her low neckline showed the swells of her breasts. The last photograph was of her wearing skin-tight jeans and high heels, her back to the camera, hands on hips and with a sexy smile as she looked over her shoulder.

"I can explain," she said in a voice so soft he barely heard her. "When I was in graduate school, a photographer friend took these of me. He wanted them for his portfolio, that's all. They were never used commercially. Sam must have taken them from my condo. He had a key because he always watered my plants whenever I went away." As though it had suddenly registered, she said, "Oh my God, he went through my things."

Chris pulled a paper with handwritten script so messy he found it hard to read. He handed it to her. "We found this. A love letter to you, Miss Moore. *To My Darling Megan,* it says.

He pours his heart out to you. You've never seen this?"

Tears formed in her eyes. "Oh, my God! No! I didn't know about this."

"Do you see how this looks?" Nick said.

"Yes, but it's not what you think. It's something else."

"What is it?" Chris asked. "Enlighten us. Detective Pulaski and I are all ears."

She fell back against the chair and crossed her arms, refusing to look at either man. Instead, she stared up at the ceiling tiles.

"I'd rather not," she said. "It's private."

"We'll come back to that," Chris said. "Let's talk about another lie you told us. You see, Miss Moore, the truth always comes back to haunt you."

"I have no idea what you're talking about."

"You told us that he worked for a military contractor in Afghanistan and that's how he lost his arm. An explosion—IED, is that right?" She nodded. "You said he installed computer equipment, set up networks. Well, we contacted the company you told us he worked for, but they have no record of Briggs working for them—ever."

"I'm not lying. Why would I lie about that?"

"Look, Miss Moore, we need to find him before the feds do. They will bring federal charges against him. They will charge him with multiple counts of murder for everything that happened in that park today. Capital murder. He could face the death penalty."

"Stop," she whispered as she covered her ears.

"Do you know where he might go if he was in trouble? A relative or friend where he might seek refuge?"

"No. He has a brother in California and a mother in a nursing home. She has Alzheimer's. No close friends."

"Except you."

"Yes, just me."

Nick asked, "Do you know his connection to Colonel Gerald Mahoney?"

"No."

Again, it was Nick who asked, "How about Jared Bolten? How did he know this guy? Did they serve together overseas?"

"I don't know anybody by that name."

"Are you sure? It's important."

"I said no!" Her outburst strangled the room into agonizing silence for a moment.

"Don't try to protect him and end up screwing him over and yourself as well," Chris said. "We're trying to help you."

"Sam is not a criminal, and I find it offensive that you talk like he is. If you only knew him."

"Oh, we plan to know everything about Sam Briggs. Do you think Detective Pulaski and I are the only ones working on this? The FBI has seized his computer, his bank account, phone records. The CMPD has dedicated an entire squad to this case. The people listed in his computer and on his phone are being contacted as we speak, and so are multiple witnesses at the shooting. Before this is over, Miss Moore, we will know more about him than you do. And we will probably learn more about you."

She covered her face with both hands and mumbled, "I can't tell you anything more, Detective Lagoni. Please. I can't! Take me home. I've been up since five this morning. I drove from Amelia Island to the Jacksonville airport. Then on to Charlotte. I'm exhausted mentally and physically. I'm sorry, I can't do this anymore." She locked eyes with him and added, "Besides, it sounds like you have all your bases covered. You don't need me."

Chris stood up. He tilted his chin at Nick who took his cue and got up. "We'll be right back."

Outside the room, Chris leaned against the wall and exhaled a deep breath. "We're not going to get anything more from her. She's shutting down. I'll drive her home and use a softer approach. I think she might go for it and open up to me. It's worth a try."

"Maybe," Nick said. "I'm beat. I'm like her—mentally and physically whipped. If you're okay, I'll leave her in your hands." Chris's mischievous smile had him adding, "Don't take that literally, Lagoni. Are you thinking what I'm thinking? Briggs will call her again. He called her a half dozen times this morning, so I think he'll call on the run. We need to coach her on what to say if he does."

"Good idea. Let's do that, and then I'll drive her home."

Chris let Nick take the lead giving her instructions for if and when Briggs called her again, most likely from a throwaway phone or from a phone booth. After Nick left to go home for a break, Chris escorted Megan down the corridor toward the elevators. Another detective from a different squad was leading a cuffed suspect to an interview room when the suspect caught sight of Megan and stopped to stare at her.

"Hi, Green Eyes," the man said with a wide grin. "Didn't think I'd see your pretty face again. Tell your man to come see me. It's been too long, know what I mean?"

Chris pushed her away from the guy and stood between them as if the man's sleaze might transfer onto her. She gazed silently back at the man with familiarity.

CHAPTER SIX

Chris was as upset with himself as with her. He had given her the benefit of the doubt, but when the street thug covered in tats and piercings knew Megan Moore, he decided it was time to play hardball. No doubt she knew the ropes. He didn't find her in the system, but he hadn't searched for an alias or street name. "Green Eyes," in all probability.

He didn't realize he had a tight grip on her arm until she winced, prompting him to release his hold. Back in the interview room again, he slung a chair away from the table and slammed it down on the floor. She sat down quickly like an obedient dog on command.

"Is there something you want to tell me, Miss Moore? You and Briggs do drugs together? That guy who spoke to you is a known drug dealer. You do business with him? Is that why you're covering for Briggs? I need answers! If you want to go home, I need answers! Are we clear?"

She didn't cower from his angry tone. In fact, she seemed unaffected, almost robotic. In a calm voice, she said, "If you take me home, detective, I promise to tell you everything. But not here." She paused as if to let him mull it over, then she said, "Legally, you can't hold me, and I don't have to talk to you at all. It's up to you. We go, and I talk. We stay, and I tell you nothing. Your choice."

"Wait here," he said, pointing his finger for her to stay seated.

He left and knocked on the door to Interview Room Two where the vice cop had taken the drug dealer. The detective stuck his head out and said, "Yeah?"

Chris said, "Let me talk to this guy, Joe. See if really does know my suspect."

"That hottie I saw you with?" he asked. Chris nodded. "Sweet! Come in."

Chris glanced at the file Joe opened for him and then extended his hand. "Mr. Harris, hi, I'm Detective Lagoni. I want to ask you a few questions." Mistrustful dark eyes stared back at him. Chris said, "That women you spoke to—how do you know her?"

"We've done business together. Wish all my customers looked like that," he said through a grin that showed a few sparse teeth stained brown. "Ain't she something?"

"How many times?"

Harris looked at the vice cop for guidance. "Answer him," Joe said forcefully. "If you cooperate, it might help your case."

"Once," said Harris, wagging his head as he stared at the tabletop. He looked up at Chris. "That's all. She was sent by one of my regulars. Her boyfriend, I guess."

"What did she buy from you?"

"I ain't tellin' you nothin'. Ask her if you want to know."

"I will, but first I'm asking you," Chris said. He eased down in the only other empty chair in the room. He slouched back and crossed his arms over his chest. "I've got all day."

"Oh, alright," the dealer said. "Oxy. She got Oxy from me. That's it." He gave Chris a mischievous grin that brought out deep lines around his hooded eyes. "Tell her to come see Pretty Boy anytime she wants. I'll take real good care of her, know what I mean?"

"You're an asshole, Harris. I hope they throw away the key when they lock you up." Chris looked over at Joe who stifled his grin. "Thanks, bro. I owe you."

Back in the room where he had left Megan, Chris stared down at her. She remained seated in the chair as if she hadn't moved a muscle. He bit down on his lower lip and continued to gaze at her, deep in thought.

"Okay, Miss Moore, let's go."

"Where?" He wondered if she thought he was locking her up in a cell.

"Home. I'm taking you home."

As he held the door open, he made a grand sweeping gesture that drew a hint of a smile from her. *Don't look too happy, Miss Moore. I'm not done with you,* he wanted to say, but kept his thoughts to himself.

§

Nick's wife came into his arms as soon as he entered the kitchen through the back door. Her swollen belly made it harder to hug her, but he stretched his arms out to envelop her. When they came apart, he ran his hand over her abdomen.

"Has the baby kicked any today?"

"Once or twice," she said with a smile. "Not like yesterday. I think last night he was doing a break dance. I couldn't even go to sleep."

He kissed her forehead and smiled, reminded of how her restlessness had kept him awake, too. He prolonged his gaze to admire her beauty. He liked her new short haircut that she described as something between a pixie and a shag. It was a drastic change from the shoulder-length style she had worn since they first met. When she had modeled the new cut for him, he told her he liked the way her blond locks framed her high cheekbones and made her blue eyes bigger, maybe even bluer. To that, she had rolled her eyes and laughed.

As she wiped her pink lipstick print off his chin, she seemed to detect his poignant demeanor, a result of the day's crisis. He'd tried to hide it from her as soon as he walked in, but his wife was too perceptive. She said, "I was worried about you, Nick, dealing with...I've been listening to the news all day since you called and told me what happened. That's all they're talking about. All the networks have their reporters on the scene. They're showing photos of some of the victims. It's so sad."

While he rested his hand on the back of his neck, he stared at the floor. "We lost one of our own, Jen. A rookie on patrol. Not even assigned to the area, just showed up when the call went out."

"I know. I saw it on TV. I'm sorry, Nick. I know you guys take this hard. It could have been you or Chris." She paused, and then said, "Speaking of Chris, have you told him yet? You were going to tell him today."

He shook his head. "I was going to, but then this happened."

"Then once this settles down. You have to tell him, honey. And soon."

"I know, I know, but he's not going to like it. That's why I've waited so long."

"It's hard because you guys have been partners for, like, forever."

"And best friends," he said. "Look, baby, I'm beat. Don't feel much like talking. I just want a beer and then sit on the patio with my wife and my dog. How about it?"

"Okay. You go on out. I'll get a beer for you and a glass of iced tea for myself."

He smiled at her, thankful for her understanding. He couldn't help internalizing his feelings, shutting her out every time he had become embedded in a tragedy where there was a death.

In the Criminal Investigation Department, it was far worse for the team when the victim was a child. One casualty of the day's shooting who still clung to life was a nine-year-old girl shot in the head. Nick thought about two recent tragedies involving a child less than four years old. Whenever the department learned a child was murdered, Captain Bowers would speak before the group with anger on his face and tears in his eyes. He'd say, "When you go home, hug your kids tonight. Tell them you love them." But before any of the guys went home, they first wanted to get their hands on the suspect who had harmed a defenseless child. They wanted to flog him, or her, into a bloody pulp, lock them up and throw away the key, and while they rotted away in prison, they prayed the lowlife got the same treatment as their victim. For anyone who preyed on a child, there was no heart for forgiveness. However, they were unable to seek revenge or get payback for the victim. They had to let the wheels of justice take over. In Nick's opinion, it sucked, but there was nothing he or any of them could do to change the system.

As soon as Nick stepped outside, their beagle pup, Barkley, jumped up on his pants legs. Nick threw Barkley's favorite ball, and while the dog went to fetch it, he stared up at a blue sky dotted with puffs of clouds. It projected a feeling of calmness and serenity, a stark contrast from the scene he had witnessed earlier that day.

He looked over his shoulder when Jennifer gently kicked the closed door with her foot to draw his attention. With their drinks in her hands, she couldn't turn the doorknob.

After he came to her aid, opening the door for her, she kissed his cheek. "Thanks. I don't know if you've heard, but they cancelled the Symphony Pops concert and the fireworks for tonight because of what happened," she said. "No one feels like celebrating. Some of the city's leaders and churches are making plans for a prayer vigil at the arena downtown. I would go with my sister, but since I'm as big as a barn, I'll stay home and watch it on television."

"I wouldn't want you out in a crowd, honey. Not after what happened," Nick said, taking a sip of his beer. After he set it down on the patio table, he reached for her and said, "C'mere, you."

He wrapped his arms around her and hugged her tightly. As many times before, he held her for an extended period of time. The tragedy of the day had heightened his gratitude for having her alive and well and in his life. When he felt the baby kick, it brought tears to his eyes.

As he continued to hold her, Jennifer said, "Forget the craziness for a while, honey. It's just you, me, and Barkley. Shut out the rest."

He nodded, but he closed his eyes and saw the bodies and blood everywhere. He heard the sobbing of loved ones. He smelled damp grass, vomit, sweat. The horror of the day would not go away.

§

Chris learned one thing about Megan Moore. She had good taste. Not that he was an expert in decorating, but her condo was cozy and neat with top-notch furnishings and decorative items. A definite upgrade from his place, but he figured a single guy who was seldom at home didn't need anything fancy.

As soon as they entered, she kicked off her sandals and tossed her purse onto a chair. He insisted on carrying her luggage to her bedroom, not necessarily because he wanted to be a gentleman, but because he wanted to check it out. He wondered if he would find any telltale signs of a relationship between her and Briggs. Men's clothing in the closet, maybe an extra toothbrush in the bathroom, or shaving cream and razor beside the sink. He saw nothing that would make him think that she shared her space, or her bed, with any man.

When he returned, he found her sitting on the sofa with her eyes closed and one leg drawn up under her. He eased down beside her but kept a respectable distance. He imagined that she was overwhelmed either because her "friend" had made a terrible mistake, or because their clandestine plans had gone awry. Chris toyed with the idea that Briggs had abandoned her to take the heat while he took off to parts unknown. Either way, he would find a way to get her to tell him. The man was at large, and Chris could find no peace until he brought him in.

Playing hardball with her would not work, he decided, so he took a different approach. He cleared his throat and said, "Is there a pizza place around here? Maybe we could order delivery. My treat."

Until their dinner arrived, Chris decided to see what was being reported on television. He reasoned that maybe it would help her understand the severity of Briggs's actions and possibly her own. They watched in silenced with Chris flipping through the channels and staying on one only long enough to learn the latest developments, according to the slant the network gave it. While Megan's eyes were on the screen, he stole glances at her, gauging her reaction to the news reports. Based on her grim expression, he felt she had finally grasped the seriousness of the situation, although he still didn't think she understood her status as a person of interest.

Thirty minutes later he put slices of pepperoni pizza on the plates she had set out. She sat at the table and waited for him to serve her, which he did. After she licked sauce off her thumb, she said, "You amaze me, detective."

"Why is that?"

"Once in a while, your hard shell cracks, and you act human."

He laughed. "Oh, really? Just part of the job—switch from being a badass to being a regular guy."

She smiled and started to say something, but her cell phone rang from inside her purse. She jumped up and ran to retrieve it before it went to voicemail. A gasp came from her when she heard a voice she recognized. As instructed earlier by Nick, she put the phone on speaker before she answered.

"Sam! Where are you?"

"Hi, Meggie. Just listen. Have to be quick. Something bad happened."

"Yes, I know. There was a shooting at Montgomery Park."

"I messed up, Meggie." She heard a moan and wondered if he was crying. "I wrestled with a man over a gun and it went off. It was an accident. I didn't know it was loaded. Cops won't buy that though. They'll think I murdered him. That's why I took off. Sorry I didn't come to pick you up."

"Come home, Sam. It'll be okay. We'll go to the police together and explain what happened. You can't stay on the run.

It'll only make things worse."

"I can't! Don't you see? I can't go to jail. No way! I'd rather die."

"Sam, just come home. Trust me on this."

"I dropped my phone, Megan. They'll come looking for me when they find it. Maybe they have my name already."

"Sam, we'll figure it out. I'm on your side. Will you come? Please."

She heard sounds in the background as though people were walking nearby. A woman's voice, a man's laughter. When the chatter died away, he said, "Okay, I'll come. Pack up some stuff, baby. We'll go away together."

"No, Sam! No! Listen to me—"

She shut her eyes and set the phone down on the foyer chest. As she struck a pose with her arms folded across her chest, she gazed up at Chris. "He hung up. I guess you heard all that. He wants me to be a fugitive with him."

"It'll never come to that. I guess I better make some calls."

She placed her hand on his arm as he drew his cell phone from his pocket. "What are you going to do?"

"Get more boots on the ground. Get ready for his visit."

"No! You can't treat him like a dangerous criminal. Look, he trusts me. I can get him to surrender. Please, detective. He's not a bad guy. He suffers from PTSD, and if you back him into a corner, he'll freak out."

Chris gave her a stern look. "You're trying my patience, Miss Moore."

CHAPTER SEVEN

When Lagoni stepped outside to make some calls and left Megan alone, she watched him from the window, but her thoughts were on Sam. "Poor Sam," she said out loud. She knew he was desperate and scared and she wanted to go to him. But how? She was being watched constantly with Lagoni underfoot and officers in unmarked cars all around the condo parking lot. She sensed their eyes on her. *Maybe while I stand at the window in full view, they're expecting me to make my move,* she thought. While she watched Detective Lagoni pacing back and forth with the phone to his ear, she reflected on the first time she had met Sam and how he had changed into what she referred to as "damaged goods."

Seven years ago. It was at a party on a cold January night, only her third date with her ex-boyfriend, Justin. He wanted to introduce her to his friends, but when they arrived, instead of doing that, he left her alone in an apartment jam-packed with strangers. A large man who looked as if he played some kind of contact sport that required serious muscle walked up to her. He wasn't as handsome as Justin, but she liked his friendly smile and the sparkle in his blue eyes. Sam's first words to her were some outrageous remark that shocked her at first, but then made her laugh. She couldn't remember what he'd said. So funny and charming, she had immediately felt drawn to him.

With Justin out of the room, he had flirted with her in a subdued matter, not overt. He told her she had beautiful eyes and her sweater brought out their color. She couldn't remember what she wore that night, but it had apparently made an impression on Sam.

After he got a little drunk, he had warned her about Justin, saying he was a womanizer who might leave her for another. In hindsight, she wished she had listened. Two months into their relationship, Justin did dump her for a tall blonde. But she and Sam remained friends, and he eventually became her neighbor when he bought the condo next to hers.

A long time ago. If only he was the same man now as he was then.

§

"I let Sam become too dependent on me. If that's a crime, then arrest me!"

Chris hadn't set out to make Megan angry. After he made his calls, he came back inside and asked her what he considered routine questions. Did she know what vehicle Briggs was driving? What kind of weapons or explosives did Briggs own? Did he owe money to anyone? Did he belong to a secret military organization with extremist views? Was she sure she'd never heard mention of Colonel Gerald Mahoney or Jared Bolten? Was Briggs mad at the world? At the government? Lastly, why was she protecting him? Did she know all along that he was going to confront Mahoney with a gun?

"I'm not answering any more of your asinine questions," she said finally.

Her shut-down and pout frustrated him to the point that he had to get up from the kitchen table and stroll over to the window, staring out at oak trees across the parking lot. When he concentrated on the spread of peach across the sky from a setting sun, it hit him that he'd forgotten a basic interrogation technique he had learned from the master: his ex-girlfriend. As an investigative reporter, Jamie Jackson had advised him to find out the person's weakness. "It's like going for the jugular. Works every time," she had said. He could still picture her shoulder shrug and the way her lips curled into a sexy smile.

Megan's weakness? Yes, he knew what it was. *Blindly and naively defending the honor of Sam Briggs, a man on the run for murder.* He'd seen it plenty of times in interviews after a murder was committed. The woman always protected "her man"—up to a point, anyway.

Chris sat back down at the table across from Megan. He put on his good-cop act and said, "Let's see if I've got this straight. Sam was badly wounded in an IED explosion in Afghanistan where he worked as a military contractor. He lost his arm, received shrapnel wounds and burns that left permanent scars, dumped by his fiancé, developed PTSD, unable to work, and denied workers' comp. Damn, that's a lot for one person to go through."

"Yes, it is," she said softly with a nod. "I met him after his deployment to Iraq and before his contract work in Afghanistan. He came back from there a different person."

"What are you saying? Iraq didn't affect him, but Afghanistan did?"

"Here's what I know—what he told me. He said that when 9/11 happened, he was so outraged, he wanted to join the military and fight the terrorists who had attacked America. He believed a lot of empty promises from an army recruiter and signed up. Eventually, he got his chance to be part of Operation Enduring Freedom.

"But he told me he came home disillusioned and disheartened. He said the American people had been duped. He had a friend who was a former CIA analyst who confided to him that her division talked themselves blue in the face trying to get the administration to understand there was no connection between Iraq and the 9/11 attacks. He began to believe that our involvement over there just stirred up a hornet's nest."

"Then why did he go back?"

"He had no plans to go back, but he got laid off from his job when the recession hit. As much as he tried, he couldn't find work. He had just bought the condo, and he needed money to pay bills. A friend told him about a contracting job in Afghanistan doing what he did here—installing computer systems, except this time for the military. It was good money—extremely good money. Of course, there was the risk, but he understood that. He was emotionally scarred by what happened in Afghanistan."

"Sure, he got blown apart by an IED and badly injured."

"There's more to it than that." After a pause, she said, "He watched two of his buddies die. He won't talk about it, but I know he has nightmares. He dreams about battles—different times, different places—although he claims he was never in any real conflicts. I've begged him to get counseling, but he won't. It's just a guess, but I think he has survivor's guilt."

She looked at the clock and drummed her polished nails on the tabletop.

"Do you think he's coming?" he asked.

"No...maybe...I don't know. I'm afraid of what might happen if he does show up. Are you going to have a shoot-out with him?"

"That's up to him. We will do everything in our power to take him alive. That's what we're trained to do."

"What if someone forgets that training?"

Chris responded with a frown. She was right. There was no way of knowing how it would go down. Tensions would be high. Briggs could be desperate, determined not to be taken alive. He hoped Briggs would go peacefully, but no one knew his state of mind. Chris knew a mixture of tensions, emotions, and guns was a recipe for disaster unless everyone involved kept their cool.

§

She almost sucked me in. You're an idiot, Chris said to himself. He was just beginning to believe Megan Moore was an innocent party, as oblivious to Briggs's misdeeds as anyone. Then Chris made two deductions that put the spotlight of suspicion back on her.

He had gone into the kitchen for a glass of water when he noted that there was a hook for keys on the wall near the back door, to the left of the light switch. There were no keys hanging from it. Back in the den, he asked her where her vehicle was parked.

When she responded that it was in the parking lot, he said, "Show me."

"Don't you believe me?" she asked.

"Let's go outside and see."

He gave her no choice. With his hand gripping her elbow, he escorted her out the front door. Like he suspected, there were no cars in her two assigned spaces. Why hadn't he noticed it when he drove up? Maybe because his eyes were on her legs instead. *Idiot!*

She couldn't even look at him when she said, "Okay, now you know Sam is in my car. He borrowed it when I went out of town because there's something wrong with his truck."

While he gave her a hard stare, he backed her against a dark red Range Rover parked next to her empty parking space. He stretched his arms forward so that his palms were flat on the side of the car with her sandwiched in between. It prevented her from escaping the brunt of his anger.

"We asked you that question twice! You told us no!"

"What you asked me was did I know what Sam was driving. I wasn't sure he was in my car, and I'm still not a hundred percent sure of that."

"You were deliberately being evasive, trying to impede our investigation. You don't want us to find him, do you?"

"No, I don't!" she said, loud enough that a neighbor walking by looked their way. She waved at the lady as if to say everything was fine. In a lower voice she said, "I told you Sam is suffering from PTSD. He can't be pushed. He's been depressed for weeks. I've been worried that he's suicidal. That's why I rushed back home. I was afraid what he might do."

"We don't need you to be a psychologist, Miss Moore. We need your cooperation."

"Screw you," she said and slipped underneath his arm.

"Hey, come back here. I'm not finished."

"I am!"

He watched her walk back to her condo, her bare feet slapping against the pavement. His focus on the sway of her hips almost made him forget his anger. Almost, but then he felt incensed at the way she disrespected his authority. He took a series of deep breaths like he had learned to do in his anger management class that the sergeant had made him attend. Back inside, he found her sitting with her legs crossed Indian-style on the sofa. Her palms were turned up and resting on her knees. Her eyes remained closed, but he was sure she was aware of his presence standing over her.

"If you must know, I'm meditating. The only way I know how to cope," she said.

"Maybe it would help your inner peace situation if you just came clean. Is there anything else you're not telling me that I should know? The reason I say that is because you are very close to being charged with obstruction of justice, Miss Moore."

She opened her eyes and said, "There's something I should tell you. My gun is missing from my drawer. So I assume Sam has it. Apparently he shot the man with my gun. In case you're interested, it's a .38 revolver." She sat up straighter and said, "Of course, he could have used my .22 that I keep in my car. I almost forgot about that."

CHAPTER EIGHT

As long as Jared stayed in his daddy's blue pickup, he had a target on his back. In his opinion, it was a piece of junk, so dumping it would not bother him any more than squashing a bug.

He parked it sixty miles to the west of Charlotte, where the countryside collided with the foothills of the Blue Ridge Mountains. The terrain afforded peaceful valleys with lakes fed from springs and rivers. Jared looked down at a lake so still it appeared untouched and untainted by mankind. The area was indeed isolated, several miles off the main highway. With no signs of development or human activity, he declared it the perfect spot to dispose of the truck.

As he made his way to the bank, he had to use caution descending the steep cliff covered in kudzu and other annoying vines with briars that scratched up his bare arms. Near the shore, he found a long limb, as thick and as strong as the pillars of a railroad trestle. It hung out over the water. He found it so sturdy that when he did a bounce test, it had no give from his weight. For balance, he extended his arms out and slowly placed one foot in front of the other. He went as far as he dared and looked down to determine the water's depth. It was dark green, a color borrowed from the neighboring trees, and murky, giving away no secrets as to what lay beneath its surface. But Jared felt certain that it was deep enough to conceal the truck. From studying the shoreline, he determined that the bank dropped off sharply, not a slow incline as some of the lakes where he went fishing.

After an arduous climb back up, he got in the pickup and closed his eyes, remembering all the times he had been in the cab with his daddy at the wheel. They'd go hunting and fishing, laughing and talking BS all the way, passing a bottle of Jack

Daniel's back and forth or sharing a tin of Skoal chewing tobacco. Happy memories for sure.

Jared removed his newly-acquired Harley motorcycle from the bed of the truck, then drove the vehicle to the very edge of the cliff so that its front tires perilously teetered on the moss-covered lip. Before he hopped out, he put the truck in neutral and released the emergency brake. With his back against the tailgate, he dug his heels in and pushed with all his might, straining so hard he felt every muscle in his body tighten. Finally, the pickup rolled forward and went over the cliff. With his hands on his hips, Jared watched as it jounced along the rugged terrain, getting scratched up along the way. It hit the water hard, producing a big splash. At first it floated, but as its open windows filled up, it sank. Nothing but the roof showed on the water's surface, and then it, too, was swallowed up by the cool mountain water.

He'd always said he was born with good brains, not like some of his crazy cousins on his mother's side of the family. No sirree, he was not a stupid redneck who did things on impulse. He was a detail guy, and he left nothing to chance. *Daddy would be proud of me,* he thought. *I always look at all the factors before I take action. Leave nothing to chance. Military training.*

Had Jared not been a thinking man, he would have been without a ride, but he had thought to bring the trusty Harley. He mounted its padded seat and turned the starter, driving off with a satisfied smile. He headed for his bunker, his safe haven. Underground and fully stocked with everything he needed for survival, it made him feel as secure as when he was a babe in his mama's arms.

§

"You're just full of surprises, Miss Moore," Chris said. "I didn't think people looking for inner peace went around packing heat, but you proved me wrong."

She remained seated on the sofa while Chris looked down at her. He found it hard to maintain a scowl when his gaze slipped to her cleavage. To his chagrin, she quickly tugged her neckline upwards and stood up.

"Don't try to figure me out, detective, because you won't. I'm complicated."

"I get that."

She crossed her arms and tilted her chin up to meet his gaze. "I knew you wouldn't find any weapons when you searched Sam's place. Like I told you, he didn't have any. When he was in one of his dark moods, I called his brother. He came from California to check on him. He found that Sam was depressed and using pain meds to get by. Ryan—that's his brother—got rid of all of Sam's guns so he wouldn't harm himself."

"Pain meds, huh? Is that how you knew the drug dealer at the police station? You bought drugs from him for Briggs?"

"Only once and only because he begged me."

"A true friend."

Megan scowled at his caustic remark. Her tone was sharp when she said, "My fear is that Sam could kill himself with my gun, or he could let you guys do it for him. Don't you see, he won't be able to live with himself after what he has done? The war itself was bad enough, but now that he has killed someone... oh, you figure it out." He held her gaze, unsure what to say. With his lack of a response, she added, "We have nothing more to discuss. I'm going to bed. You can see yourself out."

As she headed for her bedroom, he said, "I'm not leaving."

She spun around to face him. "What?" After a pause, she added, "Why not?"

"Because I need to be here if he shows up. You don't realize it, but you're in danger. Briggs is not in a rational state of mind. We don't know what he'll do."

"You underestimate my ability to reason with him. He trusts me. The others deserted him when he came back a broken man, but not me. I knew he needed a friend." She picked up her phone and stared at the display as if willing him to call. "You can go, detective. I'll be fine."

He stepped closer, gazing down at her. "I'm staying. I'll bunk on the sofa. I don't go off duty until we find him and he's safe where he belongs."

"Behind bars."

He didn't argue with her because she was right. Again, silence seemed best.

"I better keep your phone with me in case Briggs calls again. It's time I told him about his options."

"You make it sound so simple," Megan said. "Like surrendering to you will make all this go away. Okay, keep the damn phone. *Whatever!* If you need a pillow and blanket, there's some in the linen closet, top shelf. Goodnight!"

§

The *slam* of her bedroom door left no doubt of her anger. It didn't faze him one bit. He had a case to work, and he was in charge, not her. Chris settled down on the sofa and called his partner. He wanted to find out if Nick had located anyone in Briggs's life. The list they had to go on was short since most of his friends had dropped out of his life after his return from Afghanistan. The few Nick said he was able to reach informed him that they hadn't been in touch with Sam in a while. According to them, the man who came back from the war-torn country was not the same Sam Briggs they had known. He had metamorphosed into a despondent, depressed individual, unrecognizable from the lively, amicable guy they had known as Sammy.

"Good news, I've located his brother," Nick said over the phone. "He's in San Diego. Do you want to call him, or do you want me to?"

"I'll do the honors. What's his number?"

Chris called the number Nick gave him and was pleased that the phone was answered on the third ring. He could hear the sound of traffic and footfalls that seemed to indicate Briggs walking near a busy street.

"Is this Ryan Briggs?"

"Yes. Who's calling?"

"This is Detective Chris Lagoni with the Charlotte-Mecklenburg Police Department. There has been an incident with your brother, Sam."

"Hold on. Lemme go somewhere I can actually hear you." In less than a minute, he said, "Sorry 'bout that. I was walking back to my car. What was that you said? Sammy was in an accident?"

"Not exactly. He shot a man." Chris heard a muttering of sorts, a curse word or two, he thought. "Mr. Briggs, did you hear what I said?"

"Yeah, I heard. What happened?"

His even tone led Chris to believe that the brother had prepared himself for a call that would someday bring disturbing news. It had just been a matter of time.

"Your brother shot and killed a man and then fled. We're looking for him."

"Oh, God," Ryan said, his voice low and wavering. "How did this happen?"

Although omitting some particulars of the investigation, Chris explained the altercation with Colonel Mahoney. Ryan denied ever hearing mention of the man or his brother's plans to confront him.

"Wait a minute," Ryan said. "You said at the same time some psycho guy was shooting people in the park, my brother shot this Mahoney man behind the stage?"

"Yes, that's right."

"That's bizarre. I heard bits and pieces about the mass shooting on the news, but I had no idea that Sam was there, and

I sure as hell didn't know he shot someone. Damn!" After a pause, he said. "This is a lot to take in. A damn nightmare. I knew Sammy needed help, but I never thought... Oh, man, this is terrible."

Chris waited a beat before he took the conversation in a different direction. "What can you tell me about your brother's relationship with Megan Moore?"

"Megan? Why do you want to know?"

"She might be involved. She could be withholding information from the police."

"I'm not surprised. She'd do whatever she could to protect Sammy."

"Why do you say that?"

"You don't know?" Ryan said. "They're lovers. My brother told me."

"What exactly did your brother tell you, Mr. Briggs?"

"Not a whole lot, just that she's great in bed." After an uncomfortable silence stretched out, Ryan said, "Did you hear me, detective?"

"Yeah, I heard. Are you sure about that?"

"Yes, he couldn't stop gloating. Like Beauty and the Beast, if you ask me."

"Did you ever see them together? I mean, did you see any signs that would confirm that?"

"Do you think my brother was lying to me?"

"Do you think it's possible your brother was making it up? Trying to impress you maybe?"

Ryan took his time responding, making Chris feel foolish for asking the question. But then Ryan said, "No, I don't think he was lying. She was the one who called me when she was worried about him. I dropped everything to come check on him. I know one thing: Sammy thinks the world of Megan. Can't blame him though. She's special—sweet, funny, smart, and how can I say? A baby doll with moveable parts."

The remark made Chris smile. He said, "One more thing, do

you have any idea where Sam might go if he was in trouble?"

"No, not a clue."

"Well, that's all I need, Mr. Briggs. If you hear from him, try to stress the importance of turning himself in. Staying on the run only makes it harder for him."

"Do you need me to come out there? I mean, I'm busy at work, but if you think I should come, I'll make it happen. He's my brother, for God's sake. I'd do anything for—"

Chris cut him off. "That's not necessary. We'll keep in touch. Thanks for your help."

"Detective, my brother is messed up, know what I mean? What I'm saying is try to remember that when you find him. He's not a bad person, just a little off in the head. He has flashbacks and nightmares. Anyone would if they'd been through what he has."

"I'm aware of that. Don't worry, we'll do our best to bring him in safely. I promise."

"Just keep your promise, detective. That's all I'm saying."

After Chris ended the call, he stared up at the ceiling and tried to imagine Sam and Megan as a couple. But he couldn't bring himself to visualize the two being intimate. *Fantasy. Briggs's perverted twisted fantasy, that's all. Or the real deal. Nah, couldn't be true. Or could it?*

§

Chris was too keyed up to get any sleep. There was an unhinged killer on the loose who may or may not show up. What Ryan Briggs had said still weighed heavily on his mind. The brother had given credence to the possibility that Sam and Megan were lovers. But was it true or just boastful talk? Chris wasn't sure. She denied it, which meant either she was lying or Briggs was. And Chris wanted to believe the former.

Another reason sleep would not come was thinking about the beautiful woman only a short distance down the hallway, lying between cool sheets in something flimsy, no doubt, or possibly wearing nothing at all. He tried to keep his mind from wandering into lustful territory, but he was a man whose needs had not been met in a while.

No matter how he twisted or turned, he couldn't get his six-foot frame comfortable on Megan's sofa. Finally he gave up and paced the floor. An object behind a chair caught his attention. When he squatted down to pick it up, he realized it was a balled-up piece of paper. Flattened out in his hand, he discovered it was a letter to Megan from Sam Briggs. He had no right to read it. There was no search and seizure order of her property signed by a judge, but the cop in him, looking to fit pieces of the puzzle together, compelled him to read it. It was dated August 5, 2007, four years before his injury from the IED in Afghanistan. It read:

> Dear Megan,
>
> I'm in Virginia now working on a big job to install a network system at a financial corporation. We're working overtime, but I don't mind because that means more pay. It's close to midnight and I'm still awake even though I have to be up by six. Since I couldn't sleep, I decided to write this. I hope I can get the front desk girl to mail it for me. (I'm at a nice hotel with a bar and a pool, so can't complain.) You wanted to know what was inside my head, so I'll tell you with this letter. It's too hard to tell you in person. Megan, read this with an open mind and don't ask me about it later. Someday we'll talk about it, but not now, so please don't bring it up until I'm ready to talk. Here goes...
>
> I went to Iraq when we invaded that hell-hole to kick Saddam's butt. What a mess! I couldn't

believe it when buildings like the museum full of valuable historical artifacts were left unguarded and open to looters. What a tragedy. As we drove into Baghdad, we saw bodies of Iraqis along the road. The stench of that, plus open sewers, garbage, and smoke from buildings left to burn out was almost too much to bear. Some of the men I was with in Kuwait got sent to guard the oil fields because (in my opinion) that's all the American military and government cared about. I thought it was about weapons of mass destruction like they told us, but it wasn't long before I figured it out. We were there for the oil. If you thought it was to liberate the people or set up democracy, then you're wrong. We did Iran a giant favor. They wanted to destroy Saddam's regime, and we did it for them. My buddies on another deployment over there say the radical Shiites are coming over from Iran and going crazy blowing up everything in sight. Some of the Iraqi Republican Guard and Sunnis hightailed it into Syria, probably regrouping for revenge even as I write this.

I came home without a scratch. Some people wanted to shake my hand and thank me for my service. I never saw any real action because the guys we were supposed to fight set down their rifles and went home. While I was in Baghdad, I wore my uniform, carried my rifle, tried to intimidate Iraqis, threatened to shoot a few, but mostly I watched the chaos and slept and peed on Saddam's furnishings in one of his castles. We hit golf balls in his pool, laughed our asses off, and talked shit until we could go home. That was my war experience. With that said, I am very aware there were many soldiers who risked their lives in firefights or got blown up by IEDs. They are true heroes, true Americans. If they made it, their lives are changed forever. If they didn't, their loved ones' lives are changed forever. I am so glad I got out when I did.

I know there's still a lot you don't know about me. I'm a man of mystery. We haven't known each other very long, but over time you'll have me figured out. LOL! My ex-friend Justin was an idiot to dump you for Courtney. You are ten times smarter than her and also prettier. Sorry I didn't call before I left town. It was a last minute thing.

See you this weekend at Ryan's party. You better be there like you promised.

Love always,

Sam

After he finished reading the letter, Chris wadded it up and tossed it near the spot where he had found it. In his opinion, the letter wasn't exactly a love letter although it could be loosely interpreted as such, especially considering his "love always" closing. What he did learn was that Briggs had little use for the war, but he still went back overseas. Briggs was right when he wrote that he was a man of mystery. But before it was over, Chris vowed to know *everything* about the man, which included the problematic Miss Moore.

§

Chris stepped outside to wear off his nervous, sleepless energy. The dew hung thickly in the darkness as bugs skittered around the streetlights. He made small talk with undercover officers in unmarked cars who had nothing new to report. Then he tried to slip back inside the condo as quietly as possible.

With no light on inside, he made out Megan's silhouette in the doorway of her bedroom. She pushed back the tresses of her hair and walked toward him. He switched on a lamp so she could see where she was walking. He was mesmerized by her casual appearance, no makeup, and wearing sleep boxers and a loose knit top. One side had slid off her shoulder. When she caught his stare, she pushed it back in place.

"What time is it?" she asked.

"Almost two. Go back to sleep. Everything's fine."

"I thought you were Sam coming in. I guess he's not coming, is he?"

"No, I don't think so."

"What were you doing outside?" she asked.

"Just checking things out."

"You still have men outside, don't you?"

"Yes."

"This is becoming like a fortress. I don't like it."

He shrugged. "It is what it is. Why don't you go back to bed? I'm sorry I woke you."

"You didn't wake me. I couldn't sleep—worrying about Sam. Care for something to drink, detective? I think I'll fix some tea."

"Do you have coffee?"

"I think I can scrounge up some for you."

She put a kettle on to boil and left to put on a robe. When their drinks were ready, they sat across from each other at the small table where they had shared a pizza earlier. As he studied her pretty face, he realized he was leaning toward believing she was a naive young woman who had tried to help a troubled man. No doubt she was in over her head, but he wasn't sure she understood that.

There were still so many pieces of the puzzle missing. He didn't know why Briggs had targeted Colonel Mahoney. He couldn't figure out the connection and she had been no help with that. Also, he struggled to understand if Briggs knew Jared Bolten. *Maybe Calhoun is right. Too much of a coincidence that both shooters were in the same place at the same time,* he thought.

There was one particular question that continued to gnaw at him. He would find no peace until he had the answer. After he took a sip of his coffee, he asked her bluntly, "Tell me the truth about your relationship with Briggs. You seem to care a lot about him. More than a friend would."

"I told you already. Sam became dependent on me because I was the only one left who cared."

"Megan," he said, then quickly added, "May I call you Megan?" She nodded. "Look, I've spoken with Ryan, Sam's brother. He thought you and Sam were much more than friends. Sam told him you two were lovers. It would help me to know the truth."

"I told you, but you won't believe me. Look, I admit Sam wanted us to be more than friends, but I wasn't feeling it. I wasn't attracted to him. I didn't know the extent of his feelings until you showed me that letter. And now you say he told his brother we were lovers? Damn! I had no idea."

"There were more letters like the one I showed you," Chris said. "I think he was definitely into you, maybe to the point of an obsession. Did he ever try anything?" He paused, realizing she wasn't about to answer. "Sorry, forget I said that. It's none of my business."

"Maybe you should know," she said. "Sam tried to sexually assault me." She paused and he wondered if she would explain. In her next breath, she said, "Once—only once. He was drunk, and he tried to kiss me. When I pushed him away, he got angry and tore open my blouse. I slapped him and he stormed out after he punched a hole in my wall. I stayed away from him for about a week. He called up an escort service—to make me jealous, I guess. He made sure I could hear them through the wall. Eventually, I went over to see him. I didn't want this hanging over us. He apologized and we hugged and went back to being friends."

"Was this after he returned from Afghanistan?"

"Yes," she said softly, bowing her head and refusing to look at him.

"Thanks for telling me, Megan. It might be important."

"And just so you'll know, I'm not a gun nut, Chris—may I call you Chris?" she said with a smile. He nodded his permission that put them on a first-name basis. He liked the sound of that. "Okay, then—I'll start calling you Chris. So, *Chris,* if you must know, I got the guns for protection in case... Well, just in case."

"In case Briggs decided to try it again?"

"No. I had—I had a stalker. Ex-boyfriend. That's why I got the guns. But I don't have to worry about that guy anymore, so I should get rid of them. Maybe when Sam comes back."

"Don't worry about that. They'll be locked up in Property Control. What happened to the stalker guy?"

"Sam managed to beat him up despite being at a disadvantage with just one arm."

"You know Sam has a record for assault. Two barroom fights."

"Yes, I know. Who do you think bailed him out of jail?"

CHAPTER NINE
DAY TWO - SATURDAY, JULY 5, 2014

On Megan's sofa, with his feet hanging over the edge, Chris managed only a couple of hours of sleep before he was awakened by a commotion outside. He rubbed sleep from his eyes and walked to the window. When he peeked between the blinds, he saw TV satellite vans, cables coming out the backs of trucks, reporters and their assistants with cameras, and vehicles lining the street parallel to the building as far back as he could see.

"Holy shit!"

He found the remote for the TV and turned on the set. His worst fears were confirmed when he realized they were reporting Samuel Benjamin Briggs as the second shooter and Megan Allison Moore as a person of interest. As yet, they were not showing a photo of Megan, but an old mug shot of Briggs was out there for the world to see.

The network cut to a story about the deceased Colonel Mahoney and his outstanding accomplishments as a military leader. A spokesperson from the last base where he had served was interviewed. And to heighten the search for his killer, the reporter stated that Mahoney was a friend of the governor who vowed to seek justice for his fallen friend.

For the viewers who needed to be brought up to speed, a summary of the shooting the previous day was reported live by ABC's David Muir. He stood in front of the park where it had happened. The camera cut back to New York where the weekend host of *Good Morning America,* Dan Harris, highlighted the lives of some of the deceased victims of the massacre. The oldest was a seventy-year-old man and the youngest was a sixteen-year-old girl. A close-up of a nine-year-old child filled the screen. She remained in intensive care, still struggling to survive. The sight of her impish smile and bright blue eyes caused a wave of conflicting emotions for Chris. Sadness for the little girl and anger that it had happened to her.

As Chris watched, he dialed Sergeant Holden's phone number. When he picked up, Chris said, "What the fuck... How in the hell did Briggs's name get out there? And Megan Moore's? Who leaked this?"

"Calm down, Lagoni, you're yelling at the wrong person. Who do you think?"

"Right. Calhoun. He couldn't wait."

"Look, I was about to call you. Calhoun wants you there at a briefing at the FBI office. It's set for nine." Holden paused, then added, "And Lagoni, don't get him agitated, okay? We're all on the same team here."

"What about the woman? I can't leave her here alone with all the reporters outside."

"Bring her with you. Calhoun wants to question her."

"I bet he does."

"It's their show, Chris, don't forget that."

"Oh, I won't. The problem is their show is starting to look like a three-ring circus."

§

The room to the right of the living area in Megan's residence had French doors opened wide, beckoning Chris to wander inside. He flipped on a desk lamp to get a better look at his surroundings. From the time he entered her residence, he was curious about the room, and if he had a search warrant, it would have been the first place he'd focus his attention. Inside its walls were two computers and three monitors, a large desk, and two file cabinets. A mother lode of information, he assumed.

When questioned at the station, she had said she worked from home for a large investment bank and only occasionally worked from their downtown office. She stated her job title was financial analyst. She looked at them as if they had shit for brains when Nick asked what she analyzed.

"Data. Funds—for business credit. I merge reports, gather statistics, make flow charts and bar graphs, whatever is needed," she had explained.

Her desk looked innocuous enough. Unlike his work area that was a nest of chaos, hers was neat and organized. Megan apparently liked words and quotes. They were tacked on the wall with pushpins. Simple things like *Harmony, Peace, and Serenity.* A quote: *Do whatever your heart desires, but do it!* by some dude named T.X. Jones. And another that said, *Wag more, bark less.* He'd seen that one on a bumper sticker. It was the kind of thing he'd expect a New Ager like Megan to have. Just an observation he made and not a complaint. In fact, he liked it.

While he surveyed her workspace for any clues, he was unaware that she had slipped in and now stood behind him.

Her soft voice made her presence known. "What's going on outside?"

He turned around and locked eyes with her. Looking so lovely in the early morning hour, it took Chris's breath away. Her eyes, swollen with sleep, made her look childlike. So innocent looking, he thought it his duty to protect her from the vultures hovering outside.

"We have to get you out of here," he said. "Your name, as well as Sam's, has been leaked to the press. They're camped outside."

"Oh my God! Who leaked it?"

"It doesn't matter. We have to go to FBI headquarters. We'll get you out safely without having to confront those jerks out there. Don't worry, I'll figure it out. Go get dressed while I work on a plan."

"Damn. And to think I could have stayed another week in Florida. Should've listened to my parents."

Noting her playful smile, he was surprised she could be so cavalier. *If she really knew how much trouble she was in, she'd cry—or scream.* As if amused by her remark, he returned her smile and then glanced at his watch.

"We have to be there by nine, so you better get a move-on," he said.

But before she could turn to leave, there was a knock. Chris caught her arm as she started toward the door.

"I'll get it."

She conceded with a nod, but stayed on his heels as he walked to the door. He opened it only a crack to see a woman with heavy makeup, wearing Spandex crop pants and a tank top under a nearly sheer cotton shirt. Whoever she was, she had to go.

"Hello. I'm Lisa from two doors down," she said to Chris, her brow raised with interest. To Megan, she said, "Hi, sweetie. I just heard on the news. Sam? They think our Sammy would do something like that? And you're implicated? My God! What's this world coming to? Pure nonsense. Well, I can tell you won't be making the Zumba class this morning. All those crazy reporters outside. Don't worry, I'm not talking to any of them." Her attention fell back on Chris who she inspected from head to toe. "Who is this gorgeous creature?" she asked. "Megan, you didn't tell me you had a new—"

Megan cut her off. "I don't. Lisa, this is Detective Chris Lagoni. He's investigating Sam's involvement. I'd invite you in, but I have to get ready. Apparently, I'm going somewhere with Detective Lagoni."

Lisa batted lashes coated thick with black mascara. She puckered her mouth as she seemed to contemplate something. Finally, she waved her arm in the air. "Of course, of course. Then, don't let me keep you. Megan, sweetie, can you loan me that recipe I asked for?" She winked at Chris and smiled. "It won't take but a minute, detective, and then you and Megan can go about your police stuff. C'mon, Meggie, I know exactly where to find it in your drawer."

While they were gone, Chris peeked out the blinds and saw that another TV van had pulled up. He knew the station's reporter assigned to the police beat. A bulldog. Tenacious and persistent. He cursed and walked away with his hands in his pockets.

Lisa, followed by Megan, walked out of the kitchen with an index card in her hand. She tapped it against her palm. "I'll let you know if my dish is as good as yours," she said to Megan. Turning her attention to Chris, she said, "Bye, detective, maybe I'll see you around. Not that I plan to be arrested or anything. I'm thinking something social. Do you like parties?"

"Lisa, stop it! Detective Lagoni is on official business. Don't flirt with him."

"Oh, Meggie, you know I can't help it. Bye, sweetie. Hope everything is going to be okay. Don't worry about Sam. It'll all work out. Think positive."

After she left, Chris looked at Megan. He couldn't help himself. He grinned and said, "I feel like I just got hit with something and didn't see it coming."

Megan laughed. "You have no idea. Just consider yourself lucky that she had to leave in a hurry. That lady could scramble your brain."

§

Chris got the officers assigned to security detail to clear the back parking lot and barricade it. He asked for a patrol car to back up to the door leading out the rear of the condo so he and Megan could make a mad dash into the back seat and then take off for the FBI office. The plan worked without a hitch. By the time the reporters realized CMPD was driving off with their person of interest, it was too late for them to run interference.

At the FBI field office, Chris had to leave Megan with an

agent at the front desk who was waiting to escort her to an interview room. She looked at Chris with surprise as if he had handed her over to the lions to devour. What was he supposed to do? Disobey orders? He watched them make their way down the corridor with Megan looking back over her shoulder at him. His weak smile was pointless. It offered her no reassurance, and he knew it.

In a conference room where the briefing was to be held, he found Nick already seated at a long table, staring out the window. He turned around in his swivel chair as soon as Chris entered.

"Where is everyone? I thought they said nine." Chris sat down and adjusted the plush leather seat, settling down with his arms on the armrests. "Man, I wish we had chairs like this. All it needs is a lever to make it recline and I'd be asleep in seconds."

"The briefing was postponed until later," Nick said. "Calhoun wants to interview our suspect first."

"You mean Megan Moore."

"Yes."

"My gut tells me she had nothing to do with this, Nick. I think she felt sorry for Briggs. She was trying to help him. She had no idea what he was about to do—I mean, what he did."

"I hope you're right."

Chris studied his partner of six years, a time long enough to tell when something was bothering him. He knew Nick to be a morning person who rallied the troops in the early hours with witty comments and jovial laughter. But now he looked as dismal as a gray, rainy day.

"Is everything okay, Nick? Jennifer's not having problems with her pregnancy, is she?"

"No, she's great. Fine, just fine."

"Then what's eating you, man?"

"There's something I have to tell you, Chris."

"Then spill it."

After Nick told him his news, Chris shot up from his seat.

He skulked to the counter where a carafe of coffee and cups had been set out. He filled a cup slowly, deliberately, and walked back to his seat. "Smells good, doesn't it? These guys can afford the expensive stuff, not like the shit we have."

"Is that all you've got to say?" Nick pursed his lips together, showing his irritation.

"What do you want me to say, partner? You're going to be my boss. Congrats, man! You've earned it."

"I haven't given them an answer yet. I'm still considering the offer."

"What's to think about? It's a promotion. You'll make sergeant. More pay. You've got a baby on the way. Your hours will be less crazy. You deserve it. A no-brainer."

"I'll be over you, Chris. That will change our relationship."

"You gonna ride my ass?" Chris gave a little laugh.

"You're not a team player, Chris. That's why you got passed over. You do your own thing. As your partner, I'm okay with that. You're a damn good cop. The best. You solve cases, but your tactics aren't by the book. I'll be held accountable for what you do. You screw around with the rules and it'll make me look bad. That's my dilemma."

"Hey, I won't do anything to jam you up. Promise." Chris took a sip of the steaming coffee and winced when it scalded his tongue. "Take the damn promotion. Holden's leaving, and if you don't take it, they'll probably give it to that asshole Waller. If that happens, I'll have to kill him or quit. Take your pick."

"Then you're okay with this?"

"Nick, you gotta do what's best for you. I mean it."

Nick nodded as if Chris's words offered assurance. Chris had forced himself to sound upbeat. He couldn't tell his partner the truth—that from day one when Nick would run the squad, their relationship would be changed forever. No longer could they confide in personal matters to the degree they did now.

When you spend hours on a case, in a vehicle, on the road, at the computer, and you spend more time with them than family, you tell that person the most intimate thoughts that cross your mind. Deprived of sleep and food, you are loose-lipped and somehow the words spill out of your mouth before your brain kicks into gear. But you go with it and bond. As my boss, will Nick continue to be my closest friend, my confidant, my therapist? No way, Chris thought.

Chris was glad that Nick left him to sulk in silence, sipping his coffee and staring out the window. He despised change, especially when it upset the balance of nature. Chris and Nick were a team, and now that would be no more.

After an hour of awkward chit-chat and checking their phones for texts and emails, Nick and Chris looked up when the door opened. They watched as Special Agent Calhoun waltzed in with a binder tucked under his arm. The light from the fluorescent ceiling fixture reflected off his shaved head. Although he was in the middle of the biggest case of his career, he came in as fresh as bread from the oven. An impeccable dresser, Chris estimated Calhoun's shirt and tie alone cost more than his suit.

Their eyes locked as Calhoun made his way to the end of the table where he would preside over the meeting. Without a word, he plopped down in a chair. Chris's mischievous smile seemed to make Nick nervous. He shot him "the look," which Chris knew was a warning to play nice.

However, Chris said to Calhoun, "You're just in time to ruin the rest of my day."

Calhoun glared back at him, his lips set tight. "Let's clear the air once and for all, Lagoni. Get this shit out of the way."

"I don't know what you're talking about."

"Sure you do. It's been two years, but you're still pissed. Still blaming me because your case got screwed. Not my fault, Lagoni."

"Let's see if I remember correctly. We spent three weeks

working around the clock trying to gather enough evidence to charge our suspect. When we finally had what we needed, I find out he fled the country after you guys picked him up on federal charges. Never shared that little tidbit with CMPD. You questioned him and let him go. Of course, we still have an outstanding warrant for the dude, but guess what? He'll never set foot in this country again, so the victim gets no justice."

"You win some, you lose some. That's the way the game is played. Get used to it."

"Calhoun, let me tell you—"

"Chris!" Nick shouted. "Don't do this. It's not worth it." Nick turned to Calhoun. "Are we waiting for others to join us?"

"Yeah. They'll be here any minute. They're finishing up with the press conference. Hope it doesn't hurt your feelings that you two weren't invited to participate."

"Nope," Chris said. "I hate crowds, and I'm sure the stage was a little crowded."

CHAPTER TEN

So many entered the meeting room at the Charlotte field office of the FBI that more chairs had to be brought in and set along the perimeter. Chris preferred to stand, leaning one shoulder against the wall. He could tell Calhoun was in his element, in front of the group like General Patton instructing troops on an invasion by land and sea. In Chris's opinion, this was a battle for Calhoun. A battle to defeat the forces of evil and make a name for himself in the process.

Chris gave the special agent the death stare when he mentioned a possible connection between Jared Bolten and Samuel Briggs. *Bullshit!*

"Both men were at Kandahar, Afghanistan at the same time," Calhoun said to his captive audience. "Bolten was based there with the 3rd Battalion, 75th Ranger Regiment out of Fort Benning, and Briggs was employed with a military contractor called BranPoint. He was part of a private prison detail to detain and then transport combatants and suspected terrorists from Kandahar Airfield to secret detention facilities— black sites—set up in other countries. Bolten's unit would have captured individuals and handed them over to Briggs's team. Through several sources we have learned that it would have been very easy for their paths to have crossed.

"We know that Briggs killed Gerald Mahoney behind the stage at the park about the same time that Bolten fired multiple rounds from the church tower with his rifle. Mahoney was the CEO of BranPoint since his retirement from the Army in 2003. He must have recognized Briggs at the Fourth of July event. We believe Mahoney saw Briggs with a weapon and confronted him. A struggle ensued and Mahoney received a fatal wound to the chest. I have no doubt that Colonel Mahoney is a hero who stopped Briggs from killing more people."

Chris wanted to shout out what a load of crap Calhoun was feeding the group. And they seemed to swallow it, too. Every damn word of it. *Screw this,* he muttered and left the room, ignoring the stern look from his boss, Sergeant Holden. He walked down the corridor where he was told Megan was waiting to be driven home.

The look she gave him sent a warning signal: *approach female with caution.* When she stood up and came face to face with him, he almost anticipated a slap, and for what? He didn't have a clue.

"How dare you!" she said through clenched teeth.

"How dare me what?"

"You set me up! You didn't tell me Agent Calhoun was going to grill me for an hour, then send another pit bull in to finish the job. They think Sam is connected to that psycho that killed all those people! Didn't you tell them there's no way? I thought you believed me."

"You're yelling at the wrong person. I give Briggs the benefit of the doubt. I think his conflict with Mahoney had nothing to do with the sniper shootings. But try telling that to the FBI. Let's get outta here. I'll take you home."

"Honestly I don't know who I can trust. I thought I could trust you, but you handed me over to them without telling me they still think I'm a person of interest."

"What did you expect?" he said, raising his voice with ire. "I didn't bring you here for a spa treatment or a pedicure. Your association with Briggs and the fact that he has your gun and your vehicle puts you in the middle of this." He placed his hand on her elbow and gestured with his extended hand. "Let's go."

As soon as Megan and Chris stepped outside the building they were blinded by rays of sunshine and ambushed by dozens of microphones pointed at them.

Chris resisted the urge to slug the guy poking a mic in Megan's face. He firmly gripped her arm and tried his best to steer her away and toward the patrol car. With his mouth close to her ear, he said, "Whatever they ask, say *no comment.*"

Too late. Megan responded to a reporter's first question. *Aw, shit!*

§

Calhoun figured he hit all the major points in his briefing. At least his captive audience looked satisfied, so he turned the meeting over to the forensic psychologist, John Ballenger, to give a profile of Jared Henry Bolten. With the personality of an undertaker, Ballenger was a snooze, Calhoun thought, but he had to admit he put pieces of the puzzle together so that they could get a clearer picture of the shooter.

"Bolten is a loner and has a lot of anger issues," he said. "He was bullied as a child because he had a stutter. Never made friends and was a lousy student although he was considered bright. His father, Teddy, was a security guard at a mall until he was fired for using unnecessary force to detain a shoplifter. Unable to find steady work, he turned to alcohol. His wife couldn't deal with his drinking. She walked out on the whole family, leaving her husband, Jared, and his two siblings to fend for themselves. She returned years later when her husband was diagnosed with cirrhosis of the liver. She stayed to nurse him until his death, and in return he left her his house and small life insurance policy. Jared, his brother Jimmy, and his sister Joanne were upset to be cut out of the will and never forgave their mother for leaving them in the first place. Despite the man's drinking problem, Jared looked up to his dad, who was a big influence in Jared's extremist views."

"Theodore Howard Bolten is his father's full name," Calhoun interjected.

As if annoyed by the interruption, Ballenger glared at him,

then said to the group, "As I was about to say, Teddy Bolten was involved in organizing a white supremacist group called Warriors United." Ballenger paused to take a sip of water and then continued, "The group consisted of about twenty members. They liked to spend time at a makeshift firing range set up on another member's property. As a group, they also attended gun shows. Teddy Bolten made his money as a straw buyer, re-selling assault weapons, rifles, and handguns to felons and biker gang members. He was charged and sentenced to fifteen months in prison for selling to an undercover ATF officer posing as a convicted felon and gang member. He served his sentence and was out on parole when he died."

Ballenger took another sip of water and then said, "Now for more background on Jared Bolten. After high school, he joined the army and scored high enough on tests to qualify for the Ranger Assessment and Selection Program. He was a crack-shot sniper who impressed his superiors in operations in Iraq and Afghanistan. After multiple deployments and back home in the States, he walked off base one day rather than face criminal charges for misconduct in Afghanistan. He was turned in by members of his unit for taking kill shots at innocent civilians that he claimed were confirmed insurgents. When he was dishonorably discharged, his hatred of the government grew to equal that of his father's.

"As you know, this individual is considered highly dangerous. He is looking for a reason to kill people. He has sociopathic tendencies with no conscience or regard for anyone. He sees himself as a victim. As a narcissist, his desires and needs take priority over everything. That should give you an idea of who we're dealing with. Any questions?"

After Ballenger answered several questions, Calhoun stood up and said, "Okay. Thanks, John. Let's move on. I'll give details of where we stand on the investigation, where we are concentrating our search. First of all, we believe both men are off the street and holed up somewhere, maybe together. We've learned that Sam Briggs is believed to be in a black 2012 Nissan Maxima owned by a woman named Megan Moore, an acquaintance of his. He is armed, has in his possession a .38 and a .22 handgun that belong to Miss Moore. We had hoped she would give us a solid lead where to look, but after we questioned her extensively, she gave us nothing to go on.

"Like I said, no confirmed sightings lead us to believe these guys are in a hideout. We are concentrating efforts on areas we know Bolten once used for hunting. It's rough, wooded, and mountainous terrain near the North Carolina-Tennessee border. Caves and cliffs everywhere. We have local law enforcement familiar with the surroundings helping out."

For another thirty minutes, Calhoun went over the search efforts in greater detail. After answering a bombardment of questions, he dismissed everyone so he could return to questioning Megan Moore more thoroughly.

He strode back to the interview room and threw the door open, but he found himself staring into an empty room. "Where's the woman?" he shouted at his administrative assistant.

She gave him a blank stare and swallowed hard. "Gone. Didn't you say she was free to go? I thought that's what you said."

"I said no such thing! Where did she go?"

Taken aback by his anger, she answered in a timid voice, "She left with the detective."

"Damn! Lagoni! I should have known. Get him on the line and tell him to bring her back now! Never mind, I'll tell him myself."

CHAPTER ELEVEN

The patrol car turned into the parking lot. Chris cursed under his breath when he found that the media were still clustered around Megan's condo building. He asked the officer driving to drop them off in the back where the police had used their cars to block access. The officer maneuvered around the back of one vehicle, almost trading paint. Once the car stopped, Megan and Chris sprinted for the gate at Megan's back patio. He made her wait outside while he went in to clear each room. Finding no sign of trouble, he waved her in.

She kicked off her shoes and tossed her purse on the kitchen table. He still fumed about her little rant with the reporters. He figured by now it was picked up by every network in the country. All the way back to her place, he'd reprimanded her for disobeying his order.

"For the last time, I'm sorry," she said. "First you yell at me, and now you give me the silent treatment. What are you going to do? Arrest me for being an idiot?"

He didn't respond. Instead he turned away, reached for a glass from the cabinet, and filled it with tap water. He took a big gulp that puffed out his cheeks and then swallowed. Finally, he turned to face her.

"All you had to say was 'no comment'," he said. "That simple, but no, you had to tell the reporters what you thought. Bad idea. Now it's going out on their newsfeed to broadcast over and over again. Let's hope Jared Bolten didn't see it."

"So you told me already," she said with a frown. "Well, I meant every word of it."

"I'm sure you did."

"Well, I can't take it back. It's already out there."

As he held the glass in his hand, he closed his eyes.

"What are you doing?" she asked. "Why are your eyes closed?"

"I'm fantasizing about you," he said.

"What?" Her voice screeched with annoyance.

"I'm fantasizing about you with duct tape over your mouth. A beautiful sight."

"Very funny. That reporter pissed me off."

"You defend Briggs every chance you get, but you don't really know him."

He glanced down at his phone as it rang and noted that Calhoun was calling him. Ignoring the call, he slipped the phone back into his pants pocket. When he looked up at Megan, he was amused to see her lips drawn together in a tight pucker. He had no doubt that his remark had pissed her off.

She tilted her chin up and swished her hair over her shoulder. "I know him better than anyone," she said.

"No you don't. Either he lied to you, or you're lying to us. He didn't do computer work overseas, he worked black ops for a company called BranPoint, transporting terrorists to secret prisons."

"Where did you hear that?"

"The FBI. They checked."

"That doesn't sound like something he would do."

"He would for a paycheck, which he desperately needed. His job with Coltrane Industries didn't pan out. Briggs was offered the job with BranPoint, and he took it."

She exhaled deeply and said, "Okay, detective, you've brought me home safely and chewed me out. Isn't it time you get back to finding Sam and leave me in peace?"

"First I've gotta make some calls. Check in with my sergeant."

"Well, I'm going to call my parents and tell them not to pay any attention to anything the media is reporting. All lies except what I said on camera."

When she padded off in bare feet, he played back in his head what she had said to the reporter. Was it as bad as he thought, or was he just imagining how all reporters were drawn to her little meltdown like bees to buttercups? With cameras resting on their shoulders, photographers had moved in closer also.

"Miss Moore, what was your role in the shooting?" a reporter had asked.

"I had no role. I would never do such a thing!" Megan had snapped back angrily.

"Don't say another word," Chris had whispered in her ear.

"What is your relationship with Samuel Briggs?" another reporter had asked with a mic pointed at Megan's lips.

"We're friends."

"Shut up, Megan," Chris had said through clenched teeth.

"And your relationship with Jared Bolten? How long have you and Mr. Briggs planned the shootings with him?"

"I don't know Jared Bolten and neither does Sam Briggs."

Despite Chris pulling her away, Megan wouldn't let the reporter's next words go unchallenged.

The reporter had said, "According to the FBI, Bolten and Briggs are connected. Special Agent Calhoun stated in his news conference that they possibly met overseas in Afghanistan."

She resisted Chris long enough to respond. "Please do not associate Sam Briggs with that low-life lunatic. Sam is a sweet, intelligent man who would never do anything as evil as what Bolten did. Sam is a patriot who fought in Iraq and later lost his arm in Afghanistan because of an explosion. He was—no, is a courageous man, not a coward like Bolten. Sam would never befriend a whacko like that who isn't smart enough to know he'll never get away with this."

The reporter was on to another question when Chris pushed Megan forward, one hand on her arm and the other pressed flat against her back. She had turned her head to the side to say, "I can walk on my own. You don't have to use force."

"Keep moving. Don't stop. You stop and they'll be back. Move! To the car. Over there."

"You're mad, I can tell."

"You're damn right I'm mad. That was stupid, Megan. You have no idea."

"Stupid is letting you bring me here in the first place."

"Like I had a choice. C'mon, keep moving."

Memories scrambled away the minute Megan walked back into the kitchen. She gave him a little smile that rattled him. What was he supposed to do? Smile back? Wasn't he supposed to be mad at her, or was he angrier at himself for not protecting her from the media vultures?

§

Jared parked his motorcycle to the side of the diner and smiled appreciatively at a twenty-something chick wearing tight shorts and a halter top. She tilted her chin up in a haughty manner and walked briskly past him.

Stuck-up bitch. Well, honey, if you don't want guys checking you out, then don't put your tits and ass on display.

Once inside the comfort of the air conditioning, Jared slipped into the back corner booth and took the seat facing the door. *Never, ever have your back to the door,* he had learned from an army buddy who was once a sheriff's deputy. The menu was sticking out of the metal rack that held the salt and pepper shakers. He looked it over but already knew he'd order his usual: burger and fries.

A television over the front counter was giving a news report. And there he was, Jared Henry Bolten of Gastonia, North Carolina, for the whole world to see. The station used his photo from his website where he was in full dress uniform holding his rifle. *Sweet!* They gave a brief bio: former military sniper and excellent marksman. *Damn right. The best there is, folks.* Then they had to bring up all the other shit: loner, estranged from his family, anti-government, dishonorably discharged from army, fired from several odd jobs, assault on an officer, resisting arrest, disorderly conduct, and blah, blah, blah. He wanted to blast a hole in the screen with his trusty ol' Smith and Wesson .45 that was tucked under his shirt. What mattered was the fact that he had finally gotten the public's attention. He was sure there were others who felt the same way he did, that the government was too big, too controlling. The country was being turned into a socialist state. Something had to be done, and at least he had the balls to speak out. He'd inspire others to do the same. Just a matter of time.

He placed his order with a waitress with bleached blond hair and heavy makeup. She reminded him of his sister, Joanne, who he hadn't seen in over a year. The last time was when he almost snapped the neck of her boyfriend when he had him in a headlock. He would have killed him except for his sister's pleas, begging him to stop. *The son of a bitch turned her against her own brother!* He missed her even if she didn't agree with his views. She was just not aware of what was going on in the country. She was content to be a hairdresser, listening to women unload their personal problems or gossip. *As they say, ignorance is bliss.*

The news anchor reported something happening outside the FBI office in Charlotte. They were interviewing some good-looking chick. *What's she got to do with anything,* he wondered. *What in the hell is she saying?* He caught bits and pieces over the chatter of diners. Before she was done, the bitch had called him a low-life lunatic, a whacko, and a coward! *Who does she think she is, trash-talking me like that? She doesn't even know me! And I sure would like to know who in the hell this Sam Briggs dude is.* Was he trying to steal his thunder? The mission was his alone. Why was the FBI trying to link this guy with him?

This is my operation. My plan. I'm a lone warrior. Don't need no fucking help from nobody. Didn't I make myself clear, world?

CHAPTER TWELVE

Megan stared down at her cell phone. She frowned and then looked up at Chris.

"I have over twenty voice messages, and I don't want to talk to anyone but Sam."

"Are you sure you don't know where he could be?"

"Detective Lagoni, I have told you so many times that I feel like a recording."

"And I recall you saying that if you *did* know, you wouldn't tell me." He raised his voice, hoping she'd get his point.

"I made that remark because I don't want the police gunning him down."

"They want him alive, Megan. The FBI thinks Briggs will lead to Bolten."

She gave a nervous laugh and shook her head. "You can't take fiction and try to turn it into fact because it's what you want to hear. And it doesn't matter if they want him alive or not, if Sam wants to die, he'll let them take him out. Suicide by cop. No one seems to be listening to me."

The worry in her eyes did not escape his attention. In a matter of twenty-plus hours, the ordeal, the waiting, the unknown had taken a toll on her beautiful face. She had returned from a vacation, sun-kissed and rested, to be dragged into a situation for which she was ill prepared. He had a tinge of pity for her. Her concern seemed genuine, but he had a job to do. And he'd do whatever it took to find Sam Briggs even if it meant playing on the emotions of the fragile woman before him.

His voice turned soft and sympathetic when he said, "Megan, they have trained negotiators. They'll do their best to talk him out." Her lack of eye contact and her dismissive shoulder shrug bothered him. "If you're withholding information, you can be charged with obstruction of justice, aiding and abetting a fugitive. These are serious charges. He has your gun and your vehicle. The FBI is not happy about that."

"I feel like we're going around in circles," she said, taking an exasperated breath. "I probably will never convince you that I have no knowledge of what's going on, so what's the point? Why don't you just leave? I want to be alone."

Just as she said it, there was a knock at the door. Chris looked through the peephole. "Tell that to your friend. She's back."

When he opened the door, Lisa gave him a flirtatious smile. He got a good view of her breasts on full display over the top of her blouse. He stepped back to allow her entrance.

"Hello again, detective. You are about the cutest thing I've ever seen with a badge." She looked over his shoulder at Megan, who stood behind him. "Hi, Meggie. I saw you on TV. Good God! That was some drama! You told those reporters a thing or two. You go, girl."

"Ma'am, this is not a good time for Megan to have company," Chris said. "We're trying to limit her contact for her safety as well as yours. I hope you understand."

She gave him a big smile and looked him in the eyes. "I do, detective. I'll go, but first let me see your hands." She grabbed them and held them flat over her palms.

"What are you doing?" Chris said, trying unsuccessfully to pull them away from her firm grip.

"Detective, you could use a manicure. I have two salons in town. I'll do you for free. No charge. Just to show my appreciation for all you do to keep the community safe."

"Don't need it."

She stepped closer and rubbed her thumbs over the top of his hands. "Detective, lots of men get manicures. What are you afraid of? It won't hurt."

As Megan hid her smile behind her hand, Chris looked to

her for help. She said, "I think you're making Detective Lagoni uncomfortable, Lisa."

"Am I making you uncomfortable, detective? My bad. Well, I'll go, but first, Megan, I need to borrow your garlic press for that dish I'm making from your recipe. Come, we'll find it together. Oh, detective, what is that big rig outside? Is that CNN? Take a look, will ya?"

Five minutes later, Megan and Lisa came out of the kitchen and found Chris near the window. He couldn't believe that she had slipped the garlic press into the front of her top, making it hang lower and exposing more flesh. *Distracting as hell. Crazy woman.*

She gave him a big smile and said, "Bye, detective. Let me know if you change your mind about the manicure. Remember, I'll do you for free." She gave him a smile and a wink as she slipped out the door.

Relieved that she was gone, Chris turned back to the window. He had spotted no big rig like Lisa had suggested. If it was there before, it had driven off.

Megan sat down on the sofa. A loud shattering noise suddenly punctured the silent air as an object burst through the window, exploding it inwards. A big crash, so fast, so unexpected, it made Chris jump. Megan screamed. Shards of glass rained down like tiny missiles. Chris hurled himself over Megan, knocking her to the floor.

"Don't move!" he yelled.

For a second or two there was silence, then he heard voices outside, followed by sirens. He felt Megan trembling underneath him, her hands clutching his shirt. When he thought it was safe, he got to his feet and pulled her up. When she turned her head, he saw that one side of her face was bloody. He noted a big gash on her forehead and small cuts on her cheek.

While he examined her wounds, she pointed to an object on the floor. He went over and picked it up. It was a large rock with a note wrapped around it, held in place with thick string.

He removed the crinkled paper and held it up to read.

"What does it say?" Megan asked.

"Shit!" he said after he read it and balled it up in his fist.

"What does it say?"

"It says, *you will die, bitch!*"

Chris was livid. He mouthed a series of expletives he didn't want to say out loud. He ran his hands through his hair and grimaced. As he looked back at Megan, he saw a trail of blood running down her face. He pulled a handkerchief from his pants pocket and pressed it against her temple.

"I've got to take you to the ER. That gash needs stitches."

Two patrol officers stationed outside for crowd control rushed through the front door. When they saw Chris, one said, "We saw it happen. We're in pursuit. It's on the radio. Black Toyota Tundra with one occupant." When the officer saw that Megan was holding a bloody cloth to her forehead, he said to Chris, "You want me to call EMS?"

"No, I'm driving her. Secure this place. Don't let anyone in but Crime Scene."

Chris turned his attention to Megan, who was still shaken. "I'm taking you to the hospital, Megan. Grab your purse and let's go."

"Who would do this?" she asked, still trembling.

"I don't know, "Chris said, "but I promise you we'll find out."

§

Megan was in the examination room getting stitched up when Chris got a call from Sergeant Holden. "We're having a briefing at Calhoun's office in forty minutes, and you need to be there, Lagoni. He's got new leads on Bolten, and we've got the person responsible for the incident at Miss Moore's home."

"Okay. As soon as I get an officer to stay with Miss Moore, I'll be on my way."

When Chris told Megan he had to leave, she looked surprised, or perhaps disappointed. He wasn't sure, but he hoped she finally believed he was her ally and not her enemy.

"You won't be alone," Chris said. "Officer Miller will be with you, and she'll take you back to your place to get some things. We'll find somewhere safe for you to stay until this blows over."

"Where are you going?"

"I have a briefing with the investigative team, but I'll come when I can. If Briggs happens to call you, you call me. Deal?"

She gave him a weak smile. "Deal."

Chris looked up at the thick white gauze that covered a portion of her temple. "Does it hurt?" he asked.

She shook her head. "Not much."

"I should've done more to protect you."

"Hey, you didn't know some crazy person would do this."

"I gotta go. Officer Miller is right outside the door. She'll call me if anything... What I mean is, she'll contact me if I'm needed."

Megan kept her eyes locked with his as if something was on her mind. *Does she want me to stay?* he wondered. It made him hesitate. He lingered at the door.

"Everything okay, Megan?"

"What?" she said mindlessly. "Yes, fine, everything's fine. You'd better go, or you'll be late for your meeting." She waved her hand in dismissal, urging him to leave.

As he turned back on his way out, he caught her smile. That damn dazzling smile that had a way of muddling his mind.

CHAPTER THIRTEEN

A s soon as Calhoun saw Chris in the corridor on his way to the conference room, he cornered him, shoving him into an empty office and closing the door.

"What the hell, Lagoni? You don't answer your phone? No one said that woman could leave. I wasn't finished with her! We had more questions. And what was that shit outside with the reporters? Do you have any idea how much damage she's done? The damn media is having a field day. You're a loose cannon, and I'll go as far up the chain as I have to go to get you kicked off this investigation. Do I make myself clear?"

Chris's eyes narrowed with his intense irritation at Calhoun. He took a step forward and said, "What you don't seem to realize, Calhoun, is that these are two separate cases. Mass shooting is all yours—hey, you can have it, but the lone shooter belongs to CMPD. The woman has nothing, and I mean absolutely *nothing,* to do with your case, so why waste your time on her?"

"They're connected, Lagoni. Both men in Afghanistan, working together. The woman is more than likely Briggs's lover, although she won't admit it. She was at the airport to meet up with him so they could escape together as planned."

"You're grasping at straws. Nothing solid on any of that."

"Look, this is *my* investigation, and I'm the one calling the shots." When he paused, Chris wanted to pulverize Calhoun's face just to remove his sneer. "You know, I've heard all the talk about you."

"Oh yeah? What's that?"

"That you let your personal feelings get in the way of being a good cop. There was another case. Some newspaper gal you were hot for," Calhoun said. Chris wished the guy had enough sense to stop there, but he didn't. "You know, I'm sure you've noticed that Miss Moore is very attractive. I can't help but wonder if she's clouding your judgment." He gave Chris a smirk. "Lagoni, don't think with your dick, use your brain."

"Y'know, you feds are all alike," Chris said with a chuckle. "You're a bunch of useless whiners that expect the local police to clean up after you shit all over the place."

"You son of a bitch!" He pushed Chris into the wall and put his hand around his throat. He released him quickly. If he hadn't, Chris feared he would have ended up slugging him, and he could then kiss his career goodbye. Calhoun's next words confirmed as much. "You mess with me, Lagoni, and I'll have your badge."

Chris bit his tongue to squelch a comeback that would only escalate their heated discourse. *I don't work for you,* Chris wanted to remind him as he followed Calhoun into the meeting.

Nick and Sergeant Holden were already seated when Chris walked in. He nodded a greeting of sorts and took a seat across the table. Nick raised one brow in a nonverbal communication as if sensing a heated exchange between his partner and Calhoun. Chris responded with a frown.

At the start of the meeting, Calhoun uploaded images from his laptop, projecting them on the white board in the front of the room. "These photos are on Bolten's website," he said. "We have verified that the photos and two videos were made at his mother's residence. See the field in the background and the power lines? They match up with what we've seen on her property. But the video of Bolten blowing up things with homemade pipe bombs was taken elsewhere, and that's what we're interested in. Note the mountain range in the background and the bare strip where trees have been cut down and the cable running down to the base. That's a ski lift. We have narrowed down the possible search to an area near two ski resorts along the North Carolina-Tennessee border. Bolten is known to have spent time there during hunting season. Of course, we're still talking a lot of acreage. We think someone from the area will know Bolten and hopefully have had a visual within the last twenty-four hours."

"Agent Calhoun," Chief Blackwell spoke up. "Now would be the time to inform this group that we received a possible sighting of Bolten hours after the shooting about thirty miles outside of town, headed west." Despite Calhoun's sour look, the chief went on to say, "A deputy had a chance encounter with a man that could be Bolten inside a convenience store although his description doesn't match up except for his clothing. And unfortunately the video doesn't give us much to go on since the guy is always looking down, wearing a cowboy hat and sunglasses. But what's important is the fact that the deputy thinks he saw a truck parked outside that matches up to the one Bolten is believed to be driving. If only we had video of that, but wouldn't you know it, the damn camera was broke! Still, guys, this is important. Yet you made no mention of this sighting in your press conference, Calhoun. It would have helped because the city is in a panic thinking this guy is on the loose, still in Charlotte when he's most likely out of the area. It would have been nice for you to assure the public of that. We've got people afraid to leave their homes around here. It is hurting businesses. I'm getting nonstop calls, the mayor is upset, and we'll have to do a follow-up press conference on our own to do damage control."

"I didn't mention it because it's pure speculation. We don't know for sure if it was Bolten, and we don't operate on speculation, chief."

Bullshit! Of course you do. Chris wanted to say it out loud, but he couldn't without digging a deeper hole for himself. His befuddled look for Calhoun's benefit would have to suffice.

"It's reliable enough for me," Blackwell said. "The mayor and I have announced a press conference later today."

"Suit yourself," Calhoun said with a shrug. "Back to what I was saying. We know Bolten is into explosives; therefore, we should assume he's not done. A second attack, different from the first, is a possibility. Regarding what you were saying, chief, folks should be on guard and that means everywhere."

Major Lackey, sitting beside Chief Blackwell, asked, "How are we doing at contacting Bolten's siblings? He has a brother and a sister. Any success finding them?"

"The brother, Jimmy, is somewhere in Alaska," Calhoun said. "We're concentrating our efforts on the sister, Joanne, who has not been very helpful. She hasn't seen her brother in over a year and claims they are estranged. She thinks her brother is a mental case, but after questioning her, we sense some family loyalty. She doesn't seem willing to rat him out."

After Calhoun's spiel, the discussion turned to Sam Briggs. Nick gave an update on the person who threw the rock into Megan's window. "We've arrested the suspect after a car chase and foot pursuit. His name is William Wagner, but he goes by Billy. His vehicle was spotted headed north on Colony, and a chase ensued. He crashed into a light pole and took off running. Our K-9 team found him hiding underneath a house. After questioning, it turns out he considers Jared Bolten a hero, and he's a big fan. He didn't like that Miss Moore said some ugly things about his main man. He's a wannabe survivalist. Nothing more. No criminal record."

"Still, we need some protection for Miss Moore," Chris said, avoiding eye contact with Calhoun. "She was lucky this time. Maybe there's more crazies out there who want to harm her, or maybe Briggs will make a bold, stupid move to contact her."

"Sure, bring her in," Calhoun said. "We have more questions for her. She can lead us to Briggs, and Briggs can lead us to Bolten. So she will be safe here, detective, in our interview room until we are satisfied with our interrogation."

Chris glanced at Holden, who cautioned him with a stern look. Chris remained silent, leaning back in his seat to stash his hands in his pockets. Better they stay there instead of around Calhoun's throat, where he was tempted to place them.

After the meeting was adjourned, Nick caught up with Chris in the corridor. "Chris, I've got a copy of the letter from BranPoint that was sent to Briggs telling him he did not qualify for workers' comp. It was signed by Laura Rafferty. She's agreed to meet with us. Let's go see her."

"Now?"

"Yes, now. Didn't you tell me if we can shed some light on Brigg's beef with the colonel, we can separate him from the other shootings? This is our chance, man."

"Yeah, right. But I need to check on Megan first."

Nick smiled. "Now she's *Megan?* Jeez, Chris, you spend a few hours with her, and now you're on a first name basis."

"Don't start with me, Pulaski. I'm not in the mood."

"It just seems that you're getting too—"

Chris stopped in his tracks and turned to face Nick. "If I get close to Miss Moore, I get closer to finding Briggs. It's an investigation technique that will be effective in this case. It's going to take time for her to trust us. So don't make this into something it's not, Pulaski. I'm just doing my job any way I can."

"Hell, don't get pissed at me," Nick said. "And Chris, just to give you a heads up, Calhoun had a talk with the Major, Captain Bowers, and Holden about you. He wants you out."

"Let 'im try. I'm not going anywhere. Not until this is finished."

CHAPTER FOURTEEN

Jared was in a huff by the time he made it back to his bunker. He knocked the brush away from the opening and threw back the hatch. He scurried down the ladder and flung open the door of a footlocker he had bought at an army surplus store. Whiskey was the only thing that could calm him down. He filled a shot glass from a bottle of Jack and downed it in one swallow. While he stuffed a chaw of tobacco in his cheek, he stared at his arsenal of weapons, ammo, and C-4 explosives. He figured there was enough to wreak havoc on the entire city if he wanted to.

Since some asshole—Sam Briggs, is it?—wants to take credit for my action, it's damn time I raised the stakes. Prove to everyone that the shooting in the park was my deal, mine alone. That dimwit profiler on Fox News is supposed to be a genius about law enforcement, but he doesn't know shit.

Jared recalled the statement the man had made as he was interviewed: "Apparently the shootings that took place in Montgomery Park were not those of a lone wolf as first reported. He had an accomplice, Samuel Briggs, who managed to kill one man that has been identified as Colonel Gerald Mahoney."

Who the hell is Colonel Gerald Mahoney? Jared wondered. He questioned why someone would be shooting at the same time he was. *It's crazy. Doesn't make sense. Is it a trick? The feds are sneaky creatures. Maybe they're setting a trap for me. Well, I sure as hell won't take the bait.*

For the time being, the brunt of his anger was directed at Megan Moore. She had said terrible things about him on television. His father had taught him that women should keep their mouths shut. By the time he reached puberty, he'd learned that Bolten men liked their women to keep their opinions to themselves. They considered them good for four things: bearing children, cooking, cleaning, and fulfilling a man's sexual needs. In Jared's opinion, a woman like Miss Moore was a liberated bitch, spouting off when she didn't know what she was talking about. She needed to be taught a lesson, he decided. He would make her take back the awful things she had said about him.

I'll make her beg for her life. Her tears, her pleas won't do her no damn good. The minute she called me a coward and an idiot, her fate was sealed. Bitch!

He thought about the time he had forced himself on Jenny Lynn behind the rock quarry in such an isolated area no one dared to venture. As if her large breasts weren't enough, the fear in her eyes had aroused him. He tore open her blouse and ran his hands roughly over her tits, biting into one nipple until it bled. When he came inside her, he kept his hand over her mouth so that her screams wouldn't distract him. For reasons he didn't quite understand, he had to keep his eyes locked on hers until he climaxed. Her surrender, no longer fighting him, had given him power over her, an exhilarating feeling. At last she had understood that a woman was supposed to submit to a man, it was natural and a beautiful thing.

Megan Moore would learn that lesson.

§

On the ride to interview Laura Rafferty, office manager for BranPoint, Nick cursed under his breath as he had to let up on the gas pedal because of a slowdown in the flow of traffic. He turned to gauge his passenger's demeanor since what he was about to say would probably anger him.

Nick cleared his throat and said, "Uh, Chris, look, there's some stuff out there about Miss Moore's—about her hissy fit. You know, on national television, when she lost it. Just thought you should know."

Chris took his eyes off the view out the car window to gaze at his partner. However, Nick kept his focus on the road as a car in front of them came to an abrupt stop. "Come on, lady, if you're going to turn, just do it!" The heel of Nick's hand hovered over the car horn.

"What kind of stuff are you talking about, Nick?"

"Just stuff." He shrugged, still looking straight ahead. "Finally! She turns right in front of a fire truck that coulda flattened her little Fiat into a pancake. Smart move, lady, real smart."

"What kind of stuff?" Chris repeated.

"Just some shit. You know, on Twitter, Facebook, the usual."

"What are they saying?"

"Junk. Trash talk. You know."

"No, I don't know. Tell me."

"Well for instance, this one dude said, 'Megan Moore can get sassy with me. She can give me a spanking any time she wants.' Another one says, 'I like it when a pretty woman gets riled up. Gets me excited.' And that's just the tame stuff." Nick gave a nervous laugh. "Assholes, all of them."

"Yeah, who listens to that shit?" Chris ran his hand over his face. Through clenched teeth, he said, "I'd like to tell those clowns to get a life. Keep their perverted thoughts to themselves."

"Like you do," Nick said with a grin.

Chris sat up straighter and tugged at his shirt collar. "Women get a bum rap, and you know it. A man mouths off, and he's called assertive. A woman mouths off, and she's a bitch or a whore. My mom was right. When I was younger, she told me there was a double standard, but I didn't believe her."

"There's more," Nick said. "I heard from a reliable source that some of the guys in our squad are taking potshots at you after they saw the video. It shows you pushing Miss Moore away from the reporters and some are saying... Hell, it doesn't matter what they're saying. You know those idiots. Psycho. Demented to the core."

"I can guess what they're saying. Been down that road before. Don't worry. I can handle it—in my own way, on my own terms. Assholes."

"Well, here we are," Nick said as he pulled into a driveway. He gave a loud sigh as if relieved to put an end to their conversation.

They soon found out that although Laura Rafferty had agreed to meet with them, she was reluctant to answer their questions. She had refused to let them come to her office. Instead, they went to her home, a two-story brick in an upscale area of the city. She seemed to have a change of heart when they arrived, stating that she had a stressful morning due to her boss's death. Chris told her their visit couldn't wait until a more convenient time. He guessed she was in her mid-forties. From the tray stand strategically placed in front of the television with an empty plate and mug still on it, he deduced that she lived alone. She wore a simple pencil skirt and cotton blouse. Although her straight hair and light makeup were as underwhelming as her dress, Chris considered her an attractive woman.

Having more finesse and diplomacy than Chris, Nick took the lead in interviewing her. He made congenial small talk with her before sliding into the hard questions. As she sat on her sofa, she crossed her legs and twirled her foot in a tight circle. She avoided eye contact and licked her lips repeatedly. Chris knew they had hit a nerve.

"Let me see if I have this right, Miss Rafferty," Nick said. "You said Sam Briggs did not qualify for workers' comp for his injuries because he was not officially on the payroll. Is that right?"

"Yes."

"What does that mean?" Chris asked.

"Chris—"

Chris challenged Nick's attempt to shut him up with a stern look. "No, it's important. What does that mean—he wasn't on the payroll? We know that nothing was reported to the IRS. How does that work? He got paid, right?"

"He worked off the grid," Laura said tersely.

"Paid in cash? Is that what you mean?"

"Not exactly, funds were wired into an account. He was a contract worker—self-employed. His job was dangerous, so therefore, his name could not appear or the enemy would... Anyway, it's just how we do business overseas."

"He was out of luck when it came to compensation," Chris said.

Laura took an exasperated breath and said, "No, detective, not really. The company paid for his medical care when he was injured by an IED. He just lost his arm. Two other men lost their lives," she said as if that would pacify them. She continued, "We had Briggs airlifted to Germany and then to Walter Reed Hospital. He was in a medically induced coma for a while. He received treatment there for several weeks. The company took care of all of that, but once he was released, Briggs was on his own. He signed a contract and agreed to those terms. Nothing we could do."

"Is that why he came to see Colonel Mahoney at the park? To make him change his mind?" Nick asked.

She shrugged. "I guess. He called our office repeatedly, enough to be a nuisance. He refused to take no for an answer. When he showed up demanding to see the colonel, we had to call security. He made a big scene, but finally left when we threatened to call the police. I feel bad for Mr. Briggs, of course. He claims he can't find employment, and he's running out of money. But there's nothing more we can do. He should be thankful we paid his medical expenses."

"Let's see if I've got this right," Chris said, avoiding Nick's unbroken stare, which he knew was meant as a warning. "Briggs risked his life every single day in a hostile country to work for your company and came back a mess and unable to find work. And he should now be thankful that BranPoint paid his medical bills. Is that right?"

She looked at Chris like she wanted to heave hot coals over his head. After a pause to compose herself, she said, "He was well paid for his services, detective."

"I'm sure. As he should have been since your company left him to fend for himself with a broken body and a shattered mind. I looked at the stock price for your company on our way over here. You guys make a lot of profit off war."

Laura shot up from her seat and motioned for the door. "I think you gentlemen had better leave. I have nothing more to say."

On their way out, Nick's glower could have knocked Chris out cold if it had been his fist instead. Chris looked up at the sky and let out a deep sigh.

"Sorry, Nick. I knew better. Don't know what got into me. Lack of sleep, I guess."

"Go home, Chris. Take a shower and get some rest. You look like shit, and you're a pain in the ass to be around. I'm going home to my beautiful wife. We'll start fresh in the morning."

Nick was right, Chris decided as he drove home. He needed a shower and maybe a power nap. He wanted to clean up before he went to check on Megan. There was no rush, he thought, since she was in good hands with Officer Miller. By now, he hoped she was tucked away in a safe house and resting. If so, why disturb her? But just as Chris walked into his apartment, he got some news that put his shower and shave on hold.

It was a call from Officer Miller. Her voice was frantic.

"She's gone! Megan Moore is gone. I took my eyes off her for one minute, no more I swear, and she just disappeared!"

CHAPTER FIFTEEN

On July 5, Jared Henry Bolten was added to the FBI Ten Most Wanted Fugitives list. The first page of their website showed a close-up shot of Bolten from his driver's license and a photograph from his website of him in full battle gear, holding an AK-47. The description on the bulletin listed the standard data about his age, size, and race. Under remarks, it stated that he was last seen in a military jungle-camouflaged uniform and boots. According to the bulletin, he was a weapons enthusiast, expert marksman, and survivalist. He was considered to be armed and extremely dangerous. Information leading directly to his arrest was worth a $100,000 reward.

The press release by the special agent in charge in the Charlotte office of the FBI stated that charges against Bolten were twenty counts of homicide, homicide of a law enforcement officer, thirty-six counts of attempted murder, as well as federal unlawful flight to avoid prosecution. It further stated anyone with information should contact the state police, Charlotte-Mecklenburg Police, or the nearest FBI office. The switchboard to all agencies received sporadic calls of sightings from all over the country but none very credible. They seemed to be made by citizens anxious to get their hands on the reward money.

But one call in particular was taken very seriously. At 3:35 in the afternoon, one day after the shooting, a caller used his cell phone to call 9-1-1 dispatch to tell them that a man claiming to be Jared Bolten was seated at the counter next to him at a diner off I-85 in Belmont, North Carolina. He claimed the man bragged about the shooting and wished he'd hit more targets. According to the caller, the man matched the description of Bolten down to his military uniform and spit-shine boots. The man listening to the blowhard finally excused himself, saying he was going to the john, but actually stepped behind the server's drink station to call the police. When he returned to his seat and the remainder of his cheeseburger, the man was still seated, ordering another soda and as an afterthought, a side of fries to go with his fish sandwich. Then he continued to crow about how he had terrorized the city. "Actually, the whole country if you think about it," he said and took a big gulp of beer, wiping foam from his lips with the back of his hand.

The Belmont Police immediately called the FBI, but the nearest field office was in Charlotte fifteen minutes away if going 90 with lights and sirens in traffic. Special Agent Calhoun directed the local police to make the arrest and hold the suspect until they could arrive on the scene. In a show of overwhelming force, the chief of police ordered all units to respond to the Tasty Burger Grill. They descended on the small diner and caught its diners slack-jawed, wondering if someone had tried to leave without paying their check. The owner, Mabel Otis, known to be as tough as a drill sergeant, could put up a big fuss if anyone tried to sneak out without paying.

Four officers with guns drawn came up behind the suspect while he chomped down on the remainder of his fish sandwich. Ten more entered the diner and took up positions along the perimeter, waving customers toward the two exits. The caller to 9-1-1 slid off the bar stool and took cover behind the largest officer he could find. The man in military garb placed his hands on the back of his head as ordered. Officers commanded him to step down from his seat and then patted him down. He was handcuffed and led away to a patrol car. With officers surrounding the car, he sat in the backseat until Calhoun and his team appeared.

In the wait time, officers did not speak with the man, nor did he try to communicate with them. Local police ran a background and license check based on the driver's license taken from his wallet. They found nothing significant to get their adrenalin pumping. There were two speeding tickets, a charge of driving while impaired, and another for possession of an illegal substance. When Calhoun and two agents arrived, they briefed him on their findings.

"What do you mean it's not our guy?" Calhoun said in a huff to the officer in charge.

"There's some similarity alright, but his license says he's James Joseph Stanton—not Bolten. We ran it and everything matches up."

Calhoun put hands on hips and stared out into space. "Damn!"

He slid into the front seat of the patrol car and turned to face the suspect.

"State your name."

"The Easter Bunny."

"Your real name."

"Eric Rudolph."

Calhoun held up the man's driver's license through the opening in the window that separated the front seat from the back.

"Are you James Joseph Stanton?"

"Yes," he said and grinned. "But you can call me Jimmy Joe like everyone else."

"What do you know about Jared Bolten?"

"I know he shot a bunch of people, killed some of 'em."

"How do you know that?"

"I ain't stupid. I saw it on the news."

"Why did you tell the man at the diner that you did the killings?"

His eyes widened with alarm. "I was just joking with him! You mean the dude believed all that shit I was saying? Is that what this is about?" Calhoun gave him a blank stare. "I'll be damned. I thought you boys wanted me for my meth lab."

He immediately realized his mistake and clamped his mouth shut. He directed his gaze out the side window.

Calhoun smirked. "I think you confused us with the DEA, but no problem, we're sending you right over to them. Just get comfortable, Mr. Stanton, while we make the arrangements."

§

"She's gone. Megan's gone!" Officer Miller repeated over the phone as if Chris hadn't comprehended the first time she had said it. "She said she was going to put her suitcase in the patrol car, and she'd be right back. She was only out of my sight for maybe sixty seconds, no more, I'm sure of it. I stepped outside and she wasn't at the car. She just—she just disappeared. It happened so fast."

Chris let the news sink in. He ran his hand down his face and exhaled. "Damn! How could this happen? Did you see anyone around?"

"Just a couple of reporters. One news van. The others are gone now."

"And they didn't see anything?"

"No. They said they saw her come out of the house. One tried to interview her, but she refused. Then the reporter went inside the van and never saw her after that."

"I'm en route—be there in a few," Chris said.

Chris activated lights and siren so that he could whizz through traffic. He was on site in fifteen minutes flat. When he pulled in, four units were parked near the condo. Officer Miller walked over to him. When Chris got out of the car, he noted her face was drawn and pinched with distress. Her eyes were barely able to make contact with him.

"We're canvassing the area and got it out on the radio," she said. "Just her description. We don't have anything out about a vehicle. Her cell goes directly to voicemail, must be turned off."

"At this point, we don't know if she left on her own or if she was abducted," Chris said, more as a question than a statement.

"No, we don't. Sorry, Lagoni. I should have—"

"Don't, Miller. It's okay. I'm not blaming you. I'm going to check with the lady in the last unit. She's close to Megan. Maybe she knows something."

"She's not home. I called her at work—some nail salon with an unpronounceable name. She hasn't seen or heard from Megan since she came over to borrow something."

"Oh, okay then." He pulled his cell phone from his pocket. "Guess I better break the news to my sergeant."

§

Chris's entire squad showed up on site along with the captain, major, and two FBI agents who worked directly under Calhoun. Only the chief of police and the special agent were absent. It didn't take a genius to figure out that Chris had dug a hole for himself. He knew he'd be in trouble when he'd hauled Megan out of the FBI office, but he did it anyway. She was their one link to Sam Briggs, and now she was gone. Was it of her own free will or by force? Chris felt like shit, and he was also scared. Scared for her. Time was of the essence, and fast action was required. He should have never let her out of his sight. He should've protected her. *Stupid, Lagoni. You idiot!*

When Nick walked up to him, Chris said, "I'm calling it quits when this is over."

"Don't say that."

"It's better if I resign and don't give Calhoun the pleasure of getting me fired." In disgust, Chris hitched his chin at the CMPD power players, thinking his team had left him high and dry so they could kiss the feds' butts. "I see the looks I'm getting. They want to believe Calhoun has it right and not me. Maybe I'm trying to make the pieces of the puzzle fit differently than they should. I could be wrong."

"Hell, no. I believe what you do, Chris. Remember what Laura Rafferty said? Briggs had a beef with BranPoint, and specifically Mahoney. They got into a scuffle and the gun went off. Nothing to do with the mass shootings." Chris stayed silent and continued to stare down at the pavement. "Chris, listen to me," Nick said. "You've got time to make it right. Find Megan Moore. Start with that."

"Yeah, I will—somehow. Hey, you didn't make it home either, did you?"

Nick smiled. "I saw Jennifer for two minutes. Just long enough to kiss her, then I got the call."

Chris nodded. They looked on as their boss, appearing mad enough to kick a puppy, made his way over to them. Holden scratched his cheek with his thumb, a habit of his whenever he started an uncomfortable conversation. "Guys, this is not good," he said. "Looks bad, real bad. Major Lackey is pissed and he's taking heat from the FBI. And just wait until the chief weighs in. Lagoni, if you'd left that woman with those guys, none of this would have happened. It's already on the national news that she's missing. Even before we could contact her family."

"Sir, in our meeting I pointed out that she needed protection. Hell, I left her at the ER getting stitched up."

"Here's the thing, Lagoni, maybe she's fine, making her way to Briggs. Maybe she's in this with him, and you've been duped. Ever thought of that? She's a suspect, gentlemen, and we should've treated her as such."

"We didn't have anything credible to link her with Briggs's actions," Nick said. "No way to charge her. She wasn't even in the area when the shooting happened. Besides, sergeant, something bothers me about this whole thing. Something no one has talked about. No one actually saw Briggs shoot Mahoney, only run from the scene. We have the bullet, but not the gun. Not a solid case by any means."

"Nick's right," Chris said, "but back to Miss Moore. She could be in danger right now, sir. She was attacked at her apartment. There are probably more whackos out there wanting to do her harm. She's most likely a victim, not a perp."

"Find her," Holden said with firmness. "We'll see how this plays out."

Chris got the hidden meaning of his remark. Yep, if Megan was involved, then he could kiss his career goodbye. No need to wait for Calhoun to initiate his termination. But he wouldn't worry about that now. His focus was on finding Megan and finding her alive, unharmed.

CHAPTER SIXTEEN

"She wouldn't take off on her own," Chris said to Nick as they stood on the sidewalk right outside Megan's condominium. They looked on as two maintenance men worked to replace the damaged window caused by the rock. "I'm telling you someone has her. She wouldn't risk taking off, especially with her head banged up like that."

"No one saw anything, Chris. Not a single eyewitness. Wouldn't she have screamed or done something if someone took her by force?"

"Not if she couldn't." He ran his hand through his hair. "Damn! What happened here?"

His cell phone rang and he looked down and frowned when he saw Holden's name appear on the display. "Shit, probably more bad news."

"Lagoni," Holden said. "I just spoke with Miss Moore's parents. They saw the news report and they're upset big time. They'll be here as soon as they can get a flight. Just wanted to give you a heads-up because they'll want to talk to the officer assigned to her. That would be you."

"Sure. Okay. Maybe I'll have good news for them by the time they arrive."

"You better have."

The conversation ended abruptly with Chris staring out into space. He watched as another K-9 team showed up to help in the search. A police helicopter flew overhead. For the sixth time he dialed Megan's cell phone, but it went straight to voicemail.

"Nick, let's go inside her condo and check it out again. Maybe we missed something."

Signs of their early morning rush out the door were

everywhere. Megan's makeup was left out in disarray on her bathroom vanity sink. Her sleep attire and underwear were tossed into the corner of her bedroom. Unwashed mugs were left on the kitchen counter. The thin blanket Chris had used on the sofa was balled up on the floor. But there was no disturbance to the doors or windows, no evidence of a forced entry.

"Now what?" Nick asked.

"I don't know why, but something tells me to reach out to Lisa, her neighbor. Let's see if Miller can give us the name of the salon."

§

Jared decided to get a bite to eat at a little place that specialized in barbeque. He thought the joint looked more like a log cabin than a diner. His mouth watered thinking about the chopped pork sandwich and side of Brunswick stew he decided to order. He was not a regular customer, which made him feel safe. No one would recognize him. He'd come only once with another man from work, killing time when the rain shut down the construction project. He remembered that the place had a wide screen TV over the front counter, and the last time he was there it was on CNN.

His eyes stayed focused on the set while he sipped his beer. The shooting in the park was still the top news story with the search for him ongoing and involving multiple agencies. It brought a smile to his lips and a crazy temptation to yell out to the other diners, "I'm the guy they're looking for. It's me!" Of course, he wouldn't do any such thing. He felt sure that his appearance was altered enough that no one made the connection.

On the TV screen, the former FBI agent-turned-consultant who was being interviewed said the search for him was now concentrated in the mountains along the state borders of North Carolina and Tennessee. They were using foot patrol, K-9s, and helicopters with thermal imaging. It made him laugh to think they were not even warm. *Cold as ice, in fact.* He secretly boasted that he had been smart to film his fireworks show in that area to throw them off track. *Yep, I have outsmarted those highfalutin feds. Whoopee!*

Again they showed the pretty woman on the screen. It was a repeat of the video he'd seen earlier where she was giving the reporters a piece of her mind. They said her name was Megan Moore, and they reported that she was Sam Briggs's neighbor and friend. They gave the street name and showed the outside of the condominiums. He knew the area. It was somewhere he'd never afford to live, but he once did a construction project across the street. The owner of the diner switched to a different channel showing a game show, so he missed the rest of the report. He had a good mind to tell the jerk to turn it back on the news, but he didn't want to draw attention to himself. Instead he finished the rest of his sandwich and beer and thought about how Megan Moore had trashed his reputation, calling him a whacko and a coward. He was still steamed over what she'd said about him, and he stuck to his decision that she would pay for disrespecting him.

I think I'll mosey on over there and pay Miss Fancy Pants a visit.

At the moment, he was the most wanted man in America, yet no one raised a brow when he showed up at Megan Moore's residence. Jared appreciated the irony. Apparently something had just happened there and was now the main focus of law enforcement. The area was overtaken by police and their cruisers. The media was forced to move farther away behind a makeshift barricade of two marked cars parked back to back. Yellow police tape stretched around the entire perimeter of the condominium parking lot. A police helicopter circled overhead. Two K-9 dogs were brought out of a van and seemed eager to go to work.

Holy shit! What's going on?

As Jared stood there straddling his motorcycle, he took in

the whole scene and decided to abort his plan. What was he thinking? There was no way he could get to the woman, kidnap her, and torture her until she begged for forgiveness. His other plan to throw a Molotov cocktail into her front window was also a stupid idea. He decided he was nuts to consider either form of punishment. Why risk getting caught? Besides, it looked to him like someone had already beaten him to the punch. He noticed that her window was shattered. It was sitting off to the side while a new one was being installed.

He was about to leave when he noticed a policeman walking in his direction. The burly guy quickened his pace and called out to him, "Hey you, hold up!" Jared tensed up and stuck his hand in his jacket pocket around the butt of his handgun. "Show me your hands, sir," the officer said. Jared eased his hand out and smiled.

"Something wrong, officer?"

"Do you live here?"

"No, sir."

"Then clear out. This is a secure area."

As the officer walked off, Jared breathed a sigh of relief. It served as a lesson. He'd be more careful. He cranked up the motorcycle and headed out, giving the officer a little salute as he passed by.

§

Chris and Nick pulled up in front of the nail salon. Chris scanned the parking lot and said, "Lisa drives a Range Rover, but it's not here, and I didn't see it back at the condo lot either. It's dark red. You see it anywhere, Nick?"

"How come you're so sure that's what she drives?"

"I saw her putting something in it this morning when I looked out the window. And the day before, I had a little confrontation with Megan and backed her against the car. That's why I remember it so well."

"Well, it's not here, bro."

"Let's go have a chat with Lisa," Chris said.

They got out of their sedan and walked up to the entrance. Chris read the lettering on the glass door: C'est Magnifique! Nail Salon. Like the sign, the interior decor was also pink with accents of purple, so girly Chris felt strange being there.

Lisa looked shocked to see them. Her uneasiness made alarm bells go off inside Chris's head. He decided to go with a gut feeling he had, which was more like a knot in the pit of his stomach. He gave Nick a knowing look, which they had perfected over years of working together. It meant that Nick would follow his lead.

"Lisa, I thought I'd take you up on that manicure," he said. Too stunned to speak, she stood in the salon's center space with her mouth hanging open. Chris gave her a big smile and said, "You said you'd do me for free. Will you do my partner for free, too?" Noting Nick's shock, Chris tried to keep a straight face and a pretense of earnestness. He said to her, "Shall we take these two chairs?"

"I thought you'd be out looking for Megan, detective," she said. "An officer called me."

"That can wait, don't you think? May we?" he asked, sitting down at a table where he assumed manicures were done. He stretched out his hands, his palms flat on the surface.

"I guess I can fit you into my schedule," she said and gave him a weak smile.

It pleased Chris that she looked worried. "Lisa, give it up," he said, letting his eyes stay engaged with hers. "All that funny business this morning—it was a game you and Megan concocted. I get it now. Very clever," he said with a grin. "You knew it would make me uncomfortable. And if I was uncomfortable, I wouldn't follow you and Megan into the kitchen. You had plenty of time to give her the key to your car and the address to wherever Briggs is. You've been in contact with him, haven't you?"

"Of course not!"

"Then where is your car?"

Her eyes pleaded with Nick to call off the attack dog in Chris. When he stood inches from her face, she took a few steps backwards.

"You don't understand, detective. I was only trying to help."

"You are going to tell us what you know right here and now, or I'm going to handcuff you and charge you. Aiding and abetting a federal fugitive is a serious offense. Obstruction of justice. Lying to an officer in a Homeland Security crisis. I'm thinking ten years in prison." He looked back at Nick. "That's about right, isn't it, Detective Pulaski? Ten years?"

"At least," he said. "Maximum could be twenty."

"Yep, I think you're right."

"Okay, okay," she said. "If I tell you everything, then you won't charge me?"

"Not if you talk now. It's a limited offer. The clock is ticking."

"All right, I'll tell you," she said. "Sam called me because he knew the police would be focused on Megan. He's scared and he's hurt. You can't really think he meant to kill that man. It was an accident! He told me the gun just went off."

"Then he'll get his chance to explain his side of the story, but first he has to turn himself in," Chris said.

"He won't! I tried to convince him, but he said no way. He said he won't go to prison, and the police won't take him alive. He wants to die, detective. That's what he told me. That's why he begged me to tell Megan to come. He wants to see her one last time and tell her he's sorry. Then," she said and stopped. She closed her eyes and shook her head. Tears rolled down her cheeks.

"Then what, Lisa? What were you going to say?"

"Then, he's going to let you guys do it for him."

"Suicide by cop?"

"Yes. That's his plan. When I told Megan that, she said she

had to get to him to beg him not to do that. She can talk him out of it, I'm sure."

"She should have told me. *You* should have told me," Chris said.

"I promised Megan I wouldn't. She felt this was the best way to handle the situation. She said if we involved the police, it would make it worse."

"Tell us where he is," Nick said.

"I don't know."

Chris took a deep breath before he spoke. *Stay cool, no need to lose it with this woman.* Although he didn't yell at her, he let Lisa know by his tone that he wanted a satisfactory answer to his question. "Of course you know. You told Megan."

"It's the truth, I don't know. I gave Megan the address I'd written down. I don't remember it. It's somewhere in the western part of the state, I know that much. On a river near Asheville. French something or another."

"The French Broad River?"

"Yes, that sounds right. Sam said to tell her to take I-85 South, then US-74, then I don't know what."

Chris looked at Nick. "She left about an hour ago. She must be somewhere on 74 by now."

"Are you thinking what I'm thinking?" Nick said. "Hope those guys have enough fuel."

"Let's call them and see," Chris said.

Chris and Nick hurried out the door, leaving Lisa without further instructions or information. They sped back to the condo parking lot where they sought out Officer Miller. They told her what they needed. She made radio contact with Snoopy One, the CMPD helicopter that was flying overhead. The co-pilot said they had just refueled and had enough for approximately three hours. Chris and Nick did a high-five as they watched it take a dip and turn west.

Chris knew Megan wouldn't even know she was being watched. She wouldn't be able to hear the rotary blades of the helicopter. Thanks to its 10x optical zoom lens, the helicopter could monitor her every move from over a mile away.

"We'll find you, Megan. It's just a matter of time," Chris said with renewed hope.

CHAPTER SEVENTEEN

Five bullets in the revolver, ten rounds in the .22 caliber Sig Sauer, and a half pint of Jim Beam bourbon. All the supplies Sam needed, although he could use something to eat. The bag of chips and beef jerky he'd found in the kitchen pantry were long gone. He had also eaten all the canned beans, tuna, and Fruit Loops. *Where are you, Megan? What's taking you so long?*

The gash in his leg needed attention. The bleeding had stopped, but if it was not treated and bandaged, it'd get infected, he surmised, not that he cared. He didn't plan on living long enough for it to make a difference. But at the moment, it throbbed with pain. He'd injured it when he had fled and jumped over a wooden post next to some parking spaces. A rusty nailhead sticking up on the top punctured his skin and left a four-inch gash. There had been no time to stop and attend to his injury. He'd kept running until he reached Megan's car. Then he cranked it up and sped away, burning rubber.

Like when he'd first started the car, his one hand shook like a drunk in desperate need of a drink. The advantage of having only one arm, half the shaking of most folks. *Funny, Briggs.* It reminded him of the lame joke he had told Megan when she'd visited him at Walter Reed Hospital once he had come out of the coma. She had tried hard not to stare. He could tell she felt ill at ease. To make her feel more comfortable, he'd said to her, "I wasted good money on that eagle tattoo." He let his eyes drift to where his left arm had been and waited for her reaction. She froze up, unsure what to do or say, so he burst out laughing. Then she did, too. He laughed until tears rolled down his cheeks. Then he sobbed like a baby in her arms, clinging to her and soaking her blouse. She held him until he had cried himself out. Then he rested his head on the pillow and took her hand in his. They stayed that way for a long time, not speaking, but silently mourning the loss of his arm and his life as it had been.

The memory faded. He got comfortable on the floor near the window that looked out at the road. If the cops were coming, he'd see them come from that direction. The back of the house faced out toward the river. Of course, they could come by water. Maybe by both—land and water. If so, then he would be surrounded.

Megan needed to hurry. He couldn't stay there long before someone would spot him. The owners could come and find their home broken into, and him, desperate and bleeding on their floor.

Megan, please hurry!

His one big regret was bringing a gun to the event where he had learned Colonel Mahoney would be the guest of honor. Once he found out that Mahoney would be there, he left in a hurry, grabbing the gun on his way out. He hadn't bothered to check to see if it was loaded, figuring it wasn't. His unexpected appearance at the park was meant to force the colonel to speak with him. His plan called for walking up to the man without warning before he had a chance to escape. The gun was needed for intimidation purposes only. To pressure him into calling his office and approving his request for workers' comp or some kind of settlement. He had risked his life for the company, for the obscene profits they made and the stock options the colonel held as CEO. All he wanted was enough to live on since no one was hiring one-armed guys in the IT field or any other field.

If only Mahoney hadn't tried to knock the gun from his hand. He should have known the colonel would put up a fight. It stunned Sam when the gun had fired. He didn't realize he still had his finger on the trigger. The startled look on Mahoney's face was etched in his brain. The colonel fell against him and then collapsed to the ground when Sam backed away. Sam knew at that moment Mahoney was either dead or dying. Time could not erase the surreal incident from his mind. He'd killed another human being, and it was something he'd have to live with the rest of his life. Sam wasn't sure he could ever make peace with himself. Although he had been angry at Mahoney, the man certainly didn't deserve to die over a simple dispute. What weigh heavier on Sam's heart was thinking about the man's family left to grieve and all because of him. He'd created the tragedy, and he didn't want to go on living with the guilt he was forced to bear.

Sam reflected on the seconds after he'd killed Mahoney. In a panic, he took off running, and then he heard screams. Oddly, the screams were coming from a different direction. Something else had happened. He didn't wait around to find out what, but of course, he had turned on the homeowner's television and saw the breaking news.

In the zeal to get the story out, the news media were linking *him* with the sniper! And at the press conference of law enforcement officials, they said the same damn thing. If he was charged with multiple counts of murder, he could be executed for crimes he did not commit. The thought of that made him sick to his stomach. However, one thing was for sure: he would do everything in his power to prevent spending one day in jail. If that meant his death, then so be it. He had died a thousand times since he had been injured. Life itself was harder than death.

CHAPTER EIGHTEEN

The bar was packed with the after-five crowd, folks getting off work and stopping in for a brew. Jared took a seat on the only barstool available near the spot where the servers came by to pick up drinks. He angled his seat with the hopes that a certain female with large breasts would brush up against him as she stretched forward for a stack of coasters.

"Excuse me," she said with a smile.

He tipped his cowboy hat. "No problem, honey."

"You look familiar," she said. "Do I know you?"

"No, but we can change that real quick."

He thought she smiled back, but he wasn't sure since she turned quickly and walked away. He decided to ask for her phone number. Of course, he'd have to wait until the heat was off before he called her. Not looking for a serious relationship, he decided that if Busty did agree to go out with him, it would have to be a one-night stand, nothing more. Warriors like him did not become emotionally attached. Just part of the sacrifice he had to make for his country, like serving in Iraq and Afghanistan where no women and no alcohol was an ironclad rule. Now that he was back in the good ol' US of A, he wanted to make up for lost time, mixing it up with an assortment of women, picking no particular favorites. And when he had to stay holed up for a while, he'd have his girly magazines and porn videos back at the bunker to keep him entertained.

The bar music was loud, the speakers blasting a Joe Nichols song, "Tequila Makes Her Clothes Fall Off." When the voluptuous server came by for more napkins, he mouthed the lyrics to the song and gave her a big smile and wink. When she smiled back, he had no doubt that she was into him also. He decided he might not wait until his third drink. The next time she came by, he'd ask for her number, real casual like as if it didn't matter to him one way or the other. She could write it down on his napkin and he'd stash it in his jeans pocket like a trophy. *Oh, yeah!*

He happened to glance at the front door and spotted a man he thought he'd shaken from his life like dirt off his boots. With luck, the burly guy would not see him. If he did, then Jared feared big time trouble. Cops with guns drawn could be on him faster than he could blink an eye.

Mickey Dexter, known by his pals as Mickey D, was the on-again, off-again boyfriend of Jared's sister, Joanne. It had been a year since Jared had seen him in the front yard of Joanne's home, a double-wide in a trailer park. His simple request of his sister for a loan was the start of a big argument with heated profanity-laced accusations tossed back and forth like a football. He had explained he'd pay Joanne back as soon as he got his next paycheck, but Mickey managed to make it *his* business, telling Jared that his sister was not going to give him one more cent. Jared pleaded his case, stating that Joanne was *family* and should be willing to help him out. He told them he needed the money to make his truck payment, not for anything foolish. But Mickey said she'd be out two hundred bucks for good. He called Jared a loser and a cheat, asking— *no, begging*—for a beating.

Jared had been on top of Mickey quicker than a lion on a fresh kill, and he had him pinned to the ground with a knee in his back. With Mickey's head locked in a tight grip, Jared figured it would take only seconds, a quick snap of his neck, to end his life. His hand-to-hand combat training finally put to good use. In hindsight, he wished he had killed him, but his sister's bawling and pleading made him stop. He left without the money, swearing and yelling at both of them as he screeched off in his truck.

The dumbass looks the same now as he did back then. Same stupid beard as if he'd trimmed it with a dull knife. Jared cursed the logo for the New England Patriots on his ball cap. He loathed the team, always had and always would. When Mickey looked his way, Jared lowered the brim of his hat down to his brows. He turned his head to the side so that his face was not in view. To his horror, Mickey walked toward the bar, headed in his direction. *Did he see me?* Jared wondered, knowing that Mickey would have known he was a wanted man unless he'd been in a drunken stupor the last few days. If he had to, Jared was prepared to fight or shoot, but he felt confident he could get away before Mickey or anyone else called the cops. Mickey kept walking, walking, getting closer and closer, but luck was on Jared's side. A blonde, young and pretty, caught Mickey D's arm and got his attention.

"Hey, girl," Jared heard him say to her. He had that same dopey grin he had used on Jared's sister. "I'll buy you a beer, honey. Set yourself down, I wanna speak to a buddy of mine first."

"Your friend can wait. Buy me that drink now. We've got a lot of catching up to do."

Mickey chuckled. "You got that right, darlin'."

Jared watched with relief as Mickey draped his arm around the girl's shoulders and walked with her to a corner table.

There would be no third beer for Jared. Nor would there be time to get the server's phone number either. He slapped a few bills on the bar and slipped out the door. Outside he took a minute to adjust to the bright sunshine. He looked up at the cloudless sky and said, "Thank you, Jesus!" Then he slipped on his motorcycle helmet and took off, revving the throttle and kicking up dust.

§

Chris sucked at waiting.

"Pure torture," he said to Nick.

So far, the police helicopter had scanned about seventy miles of Highway 74 with no sight of the Range Rover or Megan. Chris and Nick had commandeered Miller's patrol car, using it as the communication base with Snoopy One.

While Chris stared at his cell phone screen, he said to Nick, "Tell them the roof of the Range Rover is unique. It has two panels and a hump in the back." He showed Nick the photograph from the automaker's website. "See, look here."

"They know what they're looking for, Chris. Just hang tight."

Chris pinched the bridge of his nose and closed his eyes. "Why would she think she could get away with this?"

"You can ask her that yourself when we find her."

"Better us than Calhoun. He'll lock her up—you know he will." Chris exhaled deeply and purposely bumped his head hard against the headrest. "This is driving *me* nuts."

"And you're driving me nuts," Nick said. "Tell you what, you handle the radio. I'm going to step outside and call Jennifer."

Chris watched Nick walk away with the phone up to his ear. He knew the minute Jennifer had answered because he saw Nick's big smile. *At least Nick had the distraction of a beautiful wife to keep him sane in moments like this,* he thought.

He heard a familiar voice come over the radio. "We have visual," the copilot said. "Vehicle is twenty miles east of Asheville, headed west and stationary."

"What do you mean *stationary*?" Chris asked.

"It's off the side of the highway. Looks like it has a flat rear tire on driver's side. Occupant is coming out. Female."

Until he and Nick could arrive on site, Chris gave orders to have the highway patrol detain her. He called Sergeant Holden and got the go-ahead for them to catch a ride on Snoopy Two. They'd pick her up wherever the officers took her and insist on her cooperation in leading them to Sam Briggs.

No more games, Megan Moore. I'm tired of you jerking us around. She was making it hard for Chris to be on her side.

If she kept it up, he'd wash his hands of her and deliver her personally to the FBI. And after her reaction to the interview with Calhoun, he knew she didn't want that to happen.

Twenty minutes later Nick and Chris were airborne. They learned that the highway patrol had taken Megan to the nearest police station in Asheville where she was kept in a holding cell until their arrival. Lisa's car had been put on a flatbed truck and towed to the station.

Chris wondered if Megan had been told that he was personally coming to get her. He got his answer when he walked in and noted her shock. The first words out of her mouth made him want to burst out laughing.

"Are you stalking me, detective?"

"That's a good one, Miss Moore. Yeah, I'm stalking you with a police helicopter. Worked, too. You didn't get away from me."

"Now what?" she said tersely.

"Now you tell us where Briggs is. We know you were headed to see him."

Just as she opened her mouth to speak, Nick popped his head in the doorway.

"We got it, Chris. Off the navigation system on the car. Briggs is close."

"You move in now like a bunch of cowboys and he'll let you kill him," she said. "That's his plan. Is that the way you want it to end?"

He ignored her, turning his attention to Nick. "Let's give Holden an update. Guess we have no choice but to turn it over to the feds." He directed his attention back to Megan. "By the way, your parents are worried about you. They're trying to get on a flight to come up."

She exhaled in exasperation. "I know. I spoke with them and told them I'm fine and not to come."

"Good," he said, relieved that he didn't have to deal with parents on top of everything else.

They left Megan alone while they went into an office to have a conference call with Holden, Major Lackey, Captain Bowers, Calhoun, and two other FBI agents. After a long discussion of their options, the consensus was to turn over the apprehension and arrest of Sam Briggs to the SWAT team of the Asheville FBI field office, where the special agent in charge was a personal friend of Calhoun. He voiced a strong endorsement of Special Agent John Taylor's ability to bring Briggs in without a shot being fired.

"But before we implement that plan, I'd like to confer with the director to see if he wants to deploy the TS/HRT," Calhoun said.

Are you fucking kidding me? Chris kept his thoughts to himself. Calhoun was suggesting that the director of the FBI might want to deploy the Tactical Section/Hostage Rescue Team from Quantico, Virginia. Overkill, in Chris's opinion. *Sam Briggs doesn't warrant such a response.* Again, he refrained from voicing his opinion.

"In any event, we wait until morning," Calhoun said. "Make our entrance early, before dawn. That will give us time to get everyone on board—get our best negotiator on site."

After the conference call ended, Chris noted two officers talking in hushed tones. Since he'd heard them say Megan's name, he knew it had something to do with her.

"What about Miss Moore?" he asked them.

A tall, skinny officer said, "We're going to put her in a regular cell until she can be returned to Charlotte."

"Whoa! She's not going to be locked up—not if I can help it," Chris said, his voice loud enough to draw the attention of officers milling around in the adjacent room.

"We have our orders—directly from the chief, who spoke with Special Agent Calhoun. Now if you'll quit blocking our way, sir, we'll go do our job."

"I said no!" When the officer stared at Chris's hand on his chest, Chris brought it down and stepped back. "Okay, guys, let me call Calhoun and straighten this out. Miss Moore is part of our investigation, not part of the federal case. Just chill for a while until we settle this, okay?"

The officers exchanged looks, but then conceded with a nod. "Make it quick," Skinny Cop said.

Chris went into an empty office to make his call while Nick looked on with uncertainty. "It'll be fine, Nick. Just wait. I'll make him see it our way."

"In your dreams, Lagoni. That guy will—"

Chris put his finger up to silence him when Calhoun came on the line. "Calhoun, look, we came all this way for Miss Moore and we're not leaving without her. We need her to help with the negotiations with Briggs. Just as a bystander, that's it. She can feed us key information."

"You've got balls, Lagoni, I can say that much for you," Calhoun barked. "You snatched her away when we weren't finished interrogating her. You didn't contain the situation when she went ape-shit on national television. And then she takes off to hook up with the murderer on your watch. How dare you try to weasel your way back into this investigation! She's mine now. You had your chance."

Nick paced back and forth, hands on hips, as Chris and Calhoun swapped barbs that seemed to go nowhere. Finally, Chris got Holden on the line. To Chris's relief, Holden used enough diplomacy to get the federal agent to back down.

Calhoun got in the last word. "If this comes back to bite us, Lagoni, I'll destroy you if it's the last thing I do."

Chris smiled. "You do that, Calhoun."

§

Megan looked up when Chris reentered the room. They stayed locked in a stare, neither surrendering their secret thoughts with speech. At last, he waved his hand in an upward motion, summoning her to stand. "Let's go, Miss Moore. We're leaving."

"You mean I'm free to go?"

"I didn't say that. You're being detained. Until I can get you back to Charlotte, you're staying at a hotel in Asheville. For now, I'm your prison guard, so don't try anything cute."

"This just keeps getting better and better."

CHAPTER NINETEEN

Jared was getting more pissed by the minute. He hauled his laptop to a diner that had Wi-Fi service and searched the web for the latest news. The feds still had not released his infamous "letter to America." And even worse, his website had been taken down.

Damn! Who gave the fucking FBI the right to do that? What happened to freedom of speech? This country is getting more messed up, where rights of private citizens are being taken away.

Another thing that lit his fuse was when he heard the television reporters repeatedly say he had a partner in crime, a man named Sam Briggs. *There was no way in hell I'd share my mission with somebody else. So whoever this Briggs clown is, he'd better watch out. He's toast if I ever get my hands on him.*

He'd show them all. By God, he'd make them pay. He knew he'd have to do something bigger, more spectacular than the park episode. He figured with his experience with explosives, he could hit a building just like Timothy McVeigh did in Oklahoma City. If he could manage to somehow load up enough of his explosives into the trunk of a stolen vehicle and then leave it parked in a public parking garage, all hell would break loose. He'd detonate the charge from a safe distance by cell phone like he'd learned on the Internet. Then he'd keep on walking and drive off on his Harley. *That should do it,* he thought. After that, he had no doubt they'd pay attention to his message. *Every damn American, including those tree-hugging liberals.*

§

Sam watched the sun dip behind the mountains, leaving remnants of its pinkish hue splashed across the surface of the French Broad River. If he was in a different state of mind and had his iPhone with him, he'd take a picture and show it to Megan when she arrived. She'd be proud of him for mastering the camera shot with one hand. *Another triumph she'd make a fuss over,* he thought. He calculated that enough time had passed that she should have arrived, but still there was no sight of her. Lisa was supposed to sneak her car key to Megan and put the address in the car's GPS. She even promised to fill up the gas tank.

All Megan has to do is drive to where I am, so what is taking her so long?

The wait left him emotionally drained. He stretched out on the sofa, hoping that the homeowner didn't make a surprise entrance. Deprived of sleep, he couldn't keep his eyes open any longer. He drifted back and forth from consciousness to sleep, sometimes waking and wondering where he was.

He had a dream that he was back in Afghanistan, his team surrounded by Taliban. It didn't matter how many they killed because they just kept coming. Megan was there at his side, wearing a pink dress with a strand of pearls and high heels. She handed him more ammo and said, "We're running out. This is all that's left." He tried to call for air support again, but his radio didn't work. He wanted to hug Megan just to reassure her, but he couldn't put his gun down. He couldn't stop firing because the threat was too great. In his dream, he had two arms. Whole again. Strong and athletic like when he had played football in high school. The Taliban were gaining ground, so close he could see their eyes. They were pointing at him and laughing. He turned to Megan, but she had disappeared. "Megan! Megan! Where are you?" He woke up in a sweat, screaming her name.

He wanted a drink to settle his nerves, but there was no more liquor. If only he had his pain meds because his injured leg throbbed like crazy, no end in sight. He closed his eyes again. *Megan, where are you? Please come soon.* With his head comfortable in the indention of the pillow, he thought about the first time he had met her.

It was a chilly January night on the heels of an ice storm. Every time the door to his apartment opened, the shock of the cold hit him like being splashed with ice water. People continued to come and go. It was a party, and that's what people did. By the time Megan arrived, the place was packed, the music blaring, the booze flowing. As she stood in the doorway, his eyes locked on her like a missile on a target. Justin followed her in. That was the moment Sam realized she was Justin's girl, so of course, she was hands-off. Justin relieved her of her heavy wool coat and scarf and left her standing alone while he found a place to set down their coats. Since she was someone new, Sam stepped close to introduce himself. Being known as a jokester, he said, "Hi, I'm Sam. You must be Justin's probation officer." She looked at him dumbfounded. He laughed and said, "Just kidding." Her soft laughter and easy smile made him feel warm all over despite the slap of cold air from the door's opening.

He remembered every detail of her that night, even what she had worn. Tight faded jeans and a bulky wool sweater that brought out the green in her sexy eyes. He had decided then and there that he would become her friend and when (not *if*) Justin broke her heart, he'd be there, hoping to be more than just her friend.

But by the time Justin dumped her for another, he was with Amy. In love with Amy. They even talked of marrying, but it never went further than talk. In the end, he found that Amy loved him when he was a fun-loving guy with a hunky physique and great sense of humor. When he became a man broken both physically and mentally, she could love him no longer.

But Megan was there through the pain, the suffering, the physical therapy. Even when he threw things at the wall, cursed up a blue streak, or broke down in tears. She promised to be his friend forever, but she'd never be his lover. Oh, how he wished he could change that, but he couldn't.

§

Megan was both angry and shocked to find an officer standing at the door of her hotel room. As Chris inserted the key card, he introduced her to him.

"Officer Ballard is with the Asheville Police, and he'll be here for his entire shift. So don't even think of making a break for it. You won't get pass him."

Ballard's tight smile confirmed Chris's confidence in his ability to keep her secured for the night. Megan gave them both a sharp look, tilted her chin in defiance, and walked into the room. Chris followed and set her overnight bag on the floor, the bag she was supposed to have put in Miller's patrol car, but instead stashed it in Lisa's SUV before she took off. Megan was relieved that the bag was removed from the Range Rover before it was hauled away. Then it occurred to her that in all probability, it had been searched at the precinct. It made her angry to think that officers had gone through her things.

Chris went around to check the windows near the bed and in the bathroom to make sure they were locked. Despite her eye-roll for his benefit, he pretended to ignore it. In all fairness, she knew he was just doing his job and she should appreciate his diligence.

As though satisfied that there was no threat, he said, "Looks like a nice place. You should be comfortable here."

She didn't respond, opting to keep her eyes cast down rather than meet his gaze. She dropped down onto the mattress of the king-size bed and buried her face in her hands. If he understood the garbled words out of her mouth, he pretended not to, yet she sensed his stare.

She looked up and repeated, "Nice place, but a prison cell."

"Is that what you think?"

She perceived his anger, giving her a stern look with his arms folded defensively. His police shield on his belt caught a flash of sun from the window, a reminder of his authority.

"Yes, I do. No way to live. Just go, detective. Leave me in solitary confinement."

§

Chris wasn't about to leave just because Megan ordered him to.

Oh, shit, he thought when he saw tears run down her cheeks. Nothing made him more uncomfortable than the outbreak of tears streaming down a woman's face. Unsure what he should do, he tentatively eased down on the mattress beside her.

"What's wrong?"

She shook her head in dismissal. "It's nothing."

"No, tell me."

Finally she said, "I was just thinking about Sam when he was in the hospital. The image of him lying in the bed just flashed into my mind. Sometimes that happens—out of the blue. To see him like that...I wish I could forget."

He was as surprised as she was when he placed his hand on her arm, but he left it there. "It must have been awful to see him injured."

"You can't even imagine. IV tubes, oxygen pumped into his nose, marks from shrapnel all over his body, no arm—just a bandage over the stump —burns on one side of his face, hair like a Brillo pad, eyes swollen shut. I didn't even recognize him.

"And to make matters worse, his girlfriend took one look at him and decided she couldn't deal with it. She left! Just like that." Megan snapped her fingers. "So much for true love. There's no way I could have walked away after that. He needed me, and he's needed me ever since. Now I feel I betrayed him."

Chris didn't understand what she meant by that. He reflected on how fortunate Briggs was to have this special lady in his life. He admired her loyalty and devotion to the man when others had deserted him. It was clear to Chris she had a pure heart, one that was open to embracing someone in so much pain. In his thinking, Megan was as beautiful on the inside as her outwardly appearance.

"How do you figure you betrayed him? I don't follow."

"They're going to get him tomorrow, and he'll think I'm responsible. He'll think I told the FBI where to find him."

She began to sob, her shoulders shaking as she again buried her face in her hands. He inched closer to her side. In an effort to console her, his arm went around her shoulders, his hand stroking her upper arm.

"It's not your fault, Megan."

As he held her, she said, "I know you're upset with me. I'm sorry, Chris. I wanted to find Sam before the police did—so I could get him to surrender. Lisa said he was going to let the police kill him, and I wanted to talk him out of it. He needs to know someone cares."

"You should've told me. I was worried that something bad had happened to you."

She straightened up and looked into his eyes. "Forgive me?"

His hand brushed a lock of hair from her wet cheek. He smiled. "Yes, I forgive you."

Her return smile caused an impulsive reaction from him, one he hadn't thought through. He kissed her. It was short and sweet, shut down when better judgment kicked in. He shot up from the bed and ran his hand through his hair.

When he stole a glance at her, he found that she had stacked her hands over her chest as if he had violated her. He wondered about the strange look she projected. Was it alarm, anger, or confusion?

"What are you doing?"

"I'm sorry, Megan. I shouldn't have. I mean—forget it happened, okay?"

"I will, just don't ever do that again, detective."

He was no longer Chris to her, but back to being called detective. *Oh, shit.* With his head bowed, staring at the carpet, he nodded. "I don't know what I was thinking...what came over me. I—I—look—like I said, forget it happened."

"You should go." Refusing to look at him, she straightened her knit top as if the quick kiss had caused it to get twisted.

"I'll give you some time to freshen up and then you can join us for dinner. There's a place Nick mentioned. It's within walking distance."

"No. I'll order room service."

"This place doesn't have any. Look, Megan, you have to eat, and Nick insisted that you join us. He'll think it's odd if you don't. Forget what just happened. Please." He paused and waited for her to say something—anything, really. When she didn't, he said, "I'll be back in thirty minutes. I have to shower and change clothes. In the meantime, Officer Ballard will remain just outside your door. Not that I don't trust you, but as a precaution," he said with a smile.

She looked up at him. "You brought a change of clothes?"

"Nick and I keep street clothes in the trunk of the car just in case. We brought them with us on the helicopter ride. Glad we did since we're staying overnight. Just like you, Megan, we planned ahead."

Her silent stare showed her displeasure.

§

Promptly thirty minutes later Nick knocked on her door. When she opened it and saw that he was alone, he answered the question in her eyes.

"Chris went on ahead. He's saving a table for us."

"How nice of him."

Nick gave her a pointed look, unsure why there was a hint of sarcasm in her voice. "You know, he really went to bat for you at the police station."

He let her mull over his statement in the elevator all the way down to the lobby. He repeated it as he quick-stepped ahead to hold the main door for her. She gave him a puzzled look. Her eyes stayed on him, making her miss out on the glorious blood orange sunset that had caught his attention the instant they stepped outside.

"What do you mean, detective?"

"Nick. Call me Nick, okay? Wow, what a beautiful sky."

"What do you mean he went to bat for me, Nick?"

"The FBI wanted to have you arrested and kept in a cell until they could transport you back to Charlotte. Chris told them they were crazy. He said you were part of our investigation and therefore, we would take custody of you. And then he told them you were a victim because Sam Briggs stole your car and your guns without your knowledge or permission."

"How nice of him," she said again, staring off in the distance.

"Standing his ground got him into a heap of trouble with Special Agent Calhoun. But thanks to our sergeant playing referee, Calhoun backed down."

They crossed the parking lot and walked across a median that separated the hotel from a cluster of quaint shops. They faced the mountain range where Nick got a last look at the magenta shading of the clouds from the setting sun.

Megan seemed to pause long enough to take in the view that, in his opinion, was worthy of a National Geographic photo shoot. Then she turned to him and said, "Detective Lagoni can be very tough. He has a hard shell that no one can crack. Plus, he's yelled at me more than once."

"Yeah, he's got a short fuse, but he's one of the best. There's no one I'd rather have as my partner."

"You certainly have each other's back."

"Yep, you could say that." He looked at a sign that read Mountain Mama's Bar and Grill. "Here we are. I bet Lagoni is on his second beer already."

Her brow shot up. "A bar? Really."

Nick gave a sheepish grin and shrugged. "What can I say? It's convenient."

§

Megan rolled her eyes and walked through the door he held open for her. As expected, it was dark inside. Although the band had not yet started playing, there was a party mood with patrons doing shots or chug-a-lugging beer as they mingled around the bar. The speakers blared with a country rock song by a singer she didn't recognize because her taste in music leaned in a different direction.

In the back corner, she spotted Chris. He stood up when she approached the table and held out a chair for her. She studied him in his jeans and polo shirt and said, "You guys don't look like cops tonight."

"I take that as a compliment," Chris said.

"It was."

"Oh, that's right. You don't like cops."

"And to think, here I am in a bar with two. Who would've thunk?"

CHAPTER TWENTY

J ared was furious. Nobody understood why he'd killed those people since his letter still hadn't been released to the public and his website was taken down. People should know how the military treats their soldiers after they risk their lives for the sake of freedom. The brass had hung him out to dry, treated him like a common criminal. And for what? For killing a few ragheads that they said were not the enemy, but innocent civilians.

They don't know shit. One of our interpreters turned out to be Taliban, and a few guys in the Afghan National Police were also working for the Taliban. Some others were supplying drugs, sometimes to government officials. So don't tell me I was killing innocents. As far as I'm concerned, they're all guilty of somethin'. You live in corruption long enough and you, too, get dirty. It's just a matter of time.

Jared found there was too much heat on him to risk stealing a truck to haul explosives. Yet he wanted to blow up something, *anything* to draw attention and get the truth out to the public. They had a right to know about all the lies the government had fed them.

He'd have to be careful. His picture was plastered all over television and on the Internet. Of course, he'd disguised his appearance the best he could, but still...some folks were out to be heroes, sometimes taking justice into their own hands. One wrong move, and the mission would be over. He decided to go back to his friend's house to think about his plan of action.

He found it in the same disarray he'd left it. No magic fairy had come along to pick up the wadded up fast-food wrappers or crushed beer cans. In the two weeks since his friend had gone MIA, the grass had become as high as his kneecaps. And the toilet bowl stunk to high heaven. He didn't give a damn. It wasn't his place. Besides, he just came by to watch some TV and shower because his bunker didn't have either. While he washed up, he'd think about his next move. It had to be something big enough to make the feds shit their pants. *But what?* Thinking about it almost made his brain explode.

When he was done with his shower, he felt hungry, his stomach growling something awful. His buddy had a freezer full of stuff. He was a hunter, so there had to be deer, rabbit, duck, or something tasty. Maybe even a big juicy strip steak, he hoped. Just thinking about it made his mouth water. But in order to get to the steak or deer or other goodies, he'd have to move that creepy frozen object on top, and there was no way in hell he'd do that. It gave him the heebie-jeebies every time he opened the freezer lid. Instead, he found a pizza in the refrigerator freezer and heated it up.

As he ate his supper and drank beer, he watched the evening news. He was still the lead story, but it upset him that the network he was watching had bad information. A man identified as a former FBI profiler, and now a network consultant, was saying that the real mastermind behind the shooting spree at the park was most likely the second shooter, Sam Briggs. He went on to say, "Samuel Briggs has a degree in computer science and supervised a crew of IT technicians where he worked after he returned from a tour of duty in Iraq. He was considered an outstanding leader, always fair but demanding excellence from those he supervised. It's my opinion that Bolten took orders directly from him. Briggs was at the shooting site only to create a diversion while Bolten, the expert marksman, did the shooting from the tower. Bolten doesn't strike me as capable of being the lead of this operation. Everything was planned out to a T, and that's not Bolten, who failed miserably at leadership according to men who served with him in the Army."

What the fuck? Now they're giving credit to some dude I've never even met! Shit! I acted alone as always. Unless a person is financing me or fucking me, I don't need 'em. I do just fine on my own, damn it!

Jared was too upset to finish the rest of the pizza. He threw his empty beer can at the TV and was about to shut it off, but he stopped when he saw a breaking news story interrupt a report on a broken water pipe that had flooded a street near downtown. *Crazy! They break into the news to report "breaking news." Holy shit, what was that about?*

The reporter said, "I am standing in front of Coleman's on South Boulevard." Jared knew the store, but preferred to get his supplies at its competitor, Home Depot, where the prices were cheaper. He listened closely to what the reporter was saying: "About twenty minutes ago, an explosion and fire occurred. It is believed to have caused massive casualties. We're told there was a loud blast. The explosion happened near the outdoor gardening section where several customers happened to be. A section of the building was immediately engulfed in flames, shooting up thirty feet or more into the air. And as you can see behind me, it is not yet contained.

"We're told that the initial blast shook the building and sent merchandise falling from shelves. The entire store filled up with smoke while people were scrambling to get out. Security guards directed customers to the closest exits."

Paula, the news anchor, asked the reporter on the scene, "Do the police believe this explosion is in any way connected to the shooting in Montgomery Park on July the fourth?"

"I asked that question to a CMPD spokesperson who said it was too soon to speculate on a connection. However, it is curious to note that the shooting incident happened only a few miles from this site. I have learned that police have called in Homeland Security and the FBI to investigate, along with local fire investigators. If this is indeed the work of the shooter, Jared

Henry Bolten, then the report from the FBI that he is hiding in the western part of the state will need to be reexamined. I will try to get a clarification from them as soon as possible."

Paula asked, "Do we know the extent of injuries and the number of people injured by the blast?"

"No, we don't because they are still pulling people out. As you can see, ambulances have been lining up and taking people away. Two firefighters were also treated on the scene for smoke inhalation. The police have brought in K-9 dogs, but they are awaiting the all-clear sign to go in. There is still the fear of a second explosion, so first responders are using all precautions. We will be breaking into regular programming for updates as we receive them, and a full report on this incident will be covered on the eleven o'clock news. Stay tuned to this channel to learn more. Back to you, Paula."

Fate had given Jared Bolten a solution to his problem. He didn't have to find a way to explode something to get people's attention. No sirree, he could take credit for this one, he decided. After all, some people already thought he did it. *Easy as pie.* He'd write a statement and take responsibility and once again include his letter to America. And if they refused to publish it, he'd make it clear in his note that next time he'd do something bigger, more explosive, and leave a scattering of bodies and body parts that would make them regret it.

So, motherfuckers, you better listen up.

§

Megan studied the menu posted on a board over the bar and ordered chicken wings, naked without sauce, and a small salad because it was the most nutritional thing Mountain Mama's Bar and Grill served. Chris and Nick ordered the house specialty: pork ribs and hand-cut fries. Megan caught the detectives' shared amusement when she asked for a chilled glass for her wine, not that she cared what they thought.

Some time after their food arrived, Megan observed Chris eying her over the rim of his beer mug. It made her wonder if he was thinking about the kiss. She wasn't fooled by his pretense of interest in Nick's prediction of the New York Yankees's chances in making the playoffs.

She had to admit that Chris looked nice dressed in his casual attire. The knit shirt showed off his muscular build the way his dress shirt did not. The faded jeans fit snugly around his butt. If he and Nick had concealed weapons somewhere on them, she couldn't tell.

As she set her glass down, her eyes unintentionally met Chris's. His stare told her nothing about what he was thinking at that moment. She could think of nothing other than the kiss. Her head was clouded with mixed emotions, and she wondered what she would have done if he hadn't stepped back when he did. The kiss was wrong on so many levels. He still considered her a suspect, or at least a person of interest. And she didn't trust him. At any moment, he could hand her over to the feds and wipe his hands of her.

Chris continued listening to Nick, nodding his head, but keeping his eyes on her. She thought he was jerk, pretending for his partner's sake that nothing had happened between them. While the men talked between themselves about baseball, a subject that didn't interest her, she played with food she no longer wanted and sipped her wine. With finality, she pushed her plate aside and pressed the napkin to her lips.

"Thanks for dinner," she said. "If you don't mind, I'll be heading back now."

"We'll walk back together," Nick said. "Chris and I have a conference call with the FBI field office at nine."

"Good. When you talk to them, tell them I will be the first to approach Sam," she said. "I'll talk him into surrendering. The FBI can stay down the road, and I'll bring him to them."

Chris shook his head. "Not gonna happen."

"That's the only way to avoid gunfire, guys. I can bring him in peacefully. Otherwise, he will fight to the end. He'll freak when he sees cops surrounding the property. Trust me, I know what I'm talking about."

"This is not your operation, Megan," Chris said, leaning over the table and closing the distance between them. "We're trained for this."

"I guess you're okay with Sam getting killed. You don't give a damn, do you?"

He gave her a hard stare, his jaw clenched. With a raised voice, he said, "For your information, this is not *our* operation either, and we can't say shit! The FBI is calling the shots. We're just along for the ride." Her refusal to cower angered him more. He said, "You know what? We should've let the feds take you back to Charlotte and lock you up."

"Chris—"

Chris refused to let Nick cut him off. "No, Nick, I'm right. I shoulda let them take her. I was trying to be nice, but she thinks I want her friend to die tomorrow!"

"You don't know Sam like I do!"

"And that's what I'm trying to figure out. Just how well do you know Sam Briggs? You say you're just friends, but I'm thinking he's a friend with benefits. Otherwise your undying loyalty to that guy doesn't make sense."

"How dare you! You have some nerve, detective. All you care about is moving in and ambushing him. You've had all that role-play training crap, and you're just itching to put it to use, so something simpler and nonlethal doesn't appeal to you. Sam is not a criminal. He's more scared than anything."

"Sam Briggs is an irrational, trigger-happy lunatic. By now he could have an AK-47 and be ready to spray us with bullets the minute we show up. You don't know shit, lady."

Megan snatched her purse and shot up from her seat. "You can go to hell, detective! You are more of a bastard than I thought."

"Where do you think you're going?" Chris shouted.

"Back to the hotel. I'm going to call the police station and demand they return Lisa's car to me *now!* Trying to reason with you guys is a waste of my time."

"You can't go anywhere, Megan," Nick said, not letting Chris speak first. "You're in our custody. We're responsible for you. We'll escort you back to the hotel."

"Where I'll continue to be under lock and key, huh?"

§

After they had escorted Megan back to her hotel room where Officer Ballard still stood sentry, they walked back to their own room. Once inside, Nick slammed the door shut and said, "You're an asshole, Lagoni."

With his arms crossed, Chris leaned his backside against the dresser. "Tell me something I don't know."

"What happened when you carried her bag to her room? Whatever it was, it pissed her off. And now she's *really* pissed. You never stop, do you? The shit that comes out of your mouth—"

"You're imagining things."

"The hell I am! You think I didn't feel the tension between you two at dinner? What the hell, Chris?"

"We had a misunderstanding, that's all."

"Fix it!" Nick yelled. "Although there's an officer at her door, I wouldn't put it past her to find a way to get to Briggs—and screw the whole operation for us. She took off when Miller was watching her, didn't she? You should go back and apologize and make her understand it has to be done by the book. She can't go rogue on us. Maybe you don't give a shit about having the FBI on our ass, but I do. Run interference before she does something crazy. Got it?"

"You're ordering me around? I'm the senior investigator here, Pulaski, or have you forgotten? Oh that's right. You're going to be my boss, so you're just getting into practice."

"I knew you were pissed about that." Nick plopped down on the corner of the bed to take off his shoes. He looked up at Chris. "You can't handle it."

"Take the damn promotion, Pulaski! I don't give a shit." Chris looked up at the ceiling and exhaled in exasperation. "I'm done, Nick. I'm turning in my resignation when this is over."

"Don't say that. You know you can't live without this."

"No, I think I can. Whitey asked me to come down to the coast and help him out on his boat. He's offered me a partnership when he expands. He's thinking of getting a second boat. Charter fishing is a profitable business."

Nick let his smirk speak for him. But when Chris gave an indifferent shoulder shrug, he said, "You're out of your fucking mind!" Like a missile, the shoe he held was suddenly thrown at the wall. It hit its target with a loud thump and landed sideways near the door. Chris glanced at it and then at Nick, feeling he had witnessed the equivalency of a child's temper tantrum. *Even Pulaski loses his cool every now and then,* Chris thought.

Nick seemed to get a handle on his anger and frustration. His voice softened when he said, "Charter fishing boats? What the hell do you know about boats—or fishing? That's crazy talk, and you know it."

"Whitey makes good money. It's an easier life. No one to order you around or give you a hard time. Just the ocean, the boat, and the sun. A nice life, I think."

"You're nuts. Take some time off. You've been going at it too hard. You need a break."

"I'm going soft, Nick." His blunt statement made him feel like he had just confessed to a priest. "Calhoun is right. I get too emotionally invested in my cases. It affects my work. It could end up hurting me—hurting us."

"Just don't do anything rash, Chris. You're a good cop. One of the best."

Any further discussion on the subject would have to wait. Chris's phone rang. It was the anticipated conference call with the FBI and CMPD thirty minutes ahead of schedule.

Chris cursed and said, "I guess my apology to Megan will have to wait."

CHAPTER TWENTY-ONE

By the time Jared arrived at Coleman's, police had roped off the entire parking lot. He had no choice but to park the Harley behind the back of a closed dry cleaners and walk the two blocks to the scene of the explosion. Like some others who ignored the Do Not Cross tape strung up, he ducked under it to get a closer look. Even at a distance, he picked up the acrid scent of smoke. News vans and reporters had congregated in an area at the far end of the lot, out of the way of the first responders.

Although darkness had set in hours ago, the parking lot was lit up like a stadium at game time. With hands in pockets, Jared made his way closer to the action. He approached a young cop with a baby face, a rookie, he figured. He could tell the dude was jacked up and thought about how this kid-cop had seen more action in the last two days than more seasoned cops had seen in the last five years.

He waved Jared away. "Sir, you need to get back. This is a restricted area."

"I know, but I was just wondering if I might be of any help."

"No sir, we've got it covered. Please go back. No one is allowed in this area."

"Sure, officer. Just feel so helpless. What a tragedy."

"Yep, sure is."

The cop walked away and did not look back to see if Jared was obeying his order. He was too busy answering his radio attached to a clip on his shoulder. Jared listened as the officer responded, "Copy that."

Jared contemplated a good place to leave his letter addressed: *To Whom It May Concern*. He didn't want them to find it immediately. Maybe in an hour or two, but enough time must pass so that he could be clear of the area. He'd hear about the discovery of his letter on the eleven o'clock news with the update just like local news reporter had promised.

Away from light poles and surveillance cameras, he spotted the fire chief's red and white sedan in an isolated area. The perfect place to leave the envelope. He assumed the fire chief and all his buddies were inside the building dousing hotspots and helping to look for more casualties. The last Jared heard there were three known dead and twenty injured, ranging from a broken arm to third degree burns. Due to the fireball caused by the explosion, Jared figured the deceased looked more like toasted marshmallows than human beings.

Scanning his surroundings and making sure no one was watching him, Jared approached the chief's car. He lifted the windshield wiper blade and slipped his envelope between it and the glass. With his thumbs hooked over his belt, he stared down at it, pleased that it look so innocuous, like a parking ticket or a sales flyer, yet it contained a message that would make the police sweat bullets worrying about his next move. If he could blow up a big chain store, what else was he capable of? They'd have to take him seriously now.

Jared turned the switch on the Harley and took off, laughing as he drove away and swallowing a bug he tried in vain to cough up.

§

After their conference call with the Asheville FBI field office, the detectives walked the short distance to Megan's room. When Chris asked his partner to accompany him, Nick teased him about needing backup as if responding to a dangerous situation. After they greeted Officer Ballard, who looked bored, Nick's cell phone rang. Judging by the worried look on his face, Chris wondered if something was wrong.

"It's Jennifer," Nick said. "Hope everything's okay."

"Take the call, Nick. Go back to the room. I'll handle Megan."

"You sure?"

"Yeah. Go ahead. It'll be fine."

While he watched Nick walk away with the phone to his ear, Chris knocked twice, then three times. He asked Ballard to call out to her. Just as he thought they'd have to break the door down, it flung open. She eyed them with contempt.

"I need to speak with you a minute, so let me in," Chris said. When she hesitated, he said, "Don't worry, Officer Ballard will protect you from me if necessary." Ballard fought to suppress a smile.

She stepped back to allow him entrance. Before she closed the door, Chris took note of the look she gave Ballard, as if she wanted assurance that he was just a scream away.

Chris had expected her to be dressed in the ass-hugging pants and knit top she had worn to dinner, but she had changed into an oversized T-shirt. If anything was under it, he couldn't tell.

"Why are you here?" she said.

He took note of her angry tone and knew enough to proceed with caution. Otherwise, like Nick said, he'd say more stupid stuff and piss her off more.

"To tell you that we've made arrangements with the feds. They'll let you come along if you promise to stay with the negotiating team. You'll be there to feed them information about Briggs, nothing more. We leave at five sharp, so be ready."

"Okay. Goodnight. "

She tried to walk him to the door, but he refused to budge, blocking her so that she couldn't step forward. "Wait a minute, that's not all. I want to apologize for what happened earlier," he said.

"Which incident? The kiss or what you said at dinner?"

"I'm sorry I said all that shit. When I get angry, I say things I don't mean. I'm sorry, Megan."

Because of their close proximity, he picked up the scent of her perfume. Or was it shampoo? Whatever it was, it had a clean, heady scent like sunshine and flowers that made him crazy with desire. He cast his eyes down where his gaze remained pinned on her legs. He had given them their due attention back at her apartment, when she had walked around in her short dress. But he hadn't appreciated until now how they had been kissed by the sun. Bronze, smooth, and shapely. He had the insane desire to kneel down and stroke their softness. If he did something that bold, it was sure to send him over the edge, if he didn't get slapped first.

He took his gaze off her legs and let it linger on her lovely face. *I can't even think straight. Gotta stop smiling at her. Look away, dumbass.*

She broke her silence, saying, "When you look at me like that, it's hard for me to stay mad, so stop it."

"Do you want to stay mad?"

"It's a defense mechanism, detective."

He kept smiling at her. "Well, Miss Moore, we need to break down all barriers. The last thing in the world I want is for you to stay mad at me."

"Before I forgive you, there are two things I need you to understand. First, I was in no way involved with the shootings. And secondly, I am not and have never been romantically involved with Sam. Do you believe me?"

"Yes, I do, but you've gotta understand that I had to first clear you as a suspect. That's my job. And you did some crazy things that made it difficult."

"What is your final evaluation of me, detective?"

"That you're an innocent bystander. Someone who wants to help a friend in a desperate situation."

"Are you just saying that so I'll soften?"

He laughed. "No, I mean it. And about that kiss—"

"What about it?" she said, intentionally making her tone harsh.

"I would like to retract my earlier apology. I'm not sorry it happened, Megan. Are you?"

"You call that a kiss? Hardly worth mentioning."

At first, he was taken aback until she broke into a smile. "I can do better."

"Prove it, detective."

He pulled her roughly against him, her breasts pressed into his chest and her hands on his arms. "I want to hold you, to kiss you—damned to hell everything else."

"What about your job, detective? Getting involved...a suspect...it's not professional."

"You have tormented me—no, *tortured* me since we first met, Miss Moore, and that's the only crime you've committed."

Chris pressed his lips against hers. He heard her gasp and then moan as she surrendered to him. His hands moved to cover her breasts, squeezing and kneading their firmness before both hands took a trip south. They splayed out across her bottom, pressing her even tighter against him. His strong desire for her was now set on a no-turning-back course. Thoughts of job security, better judgment, were annihilated. Nothing mattered to him but having her completely.

His hands explored wherever her flesh was exposed. With his fingers, he tugged at the too-high neckline of her T-shirt, almost stretching it out of shape. He pulled it down far enough to press his lips to the warmth of her neck. He then gave her a bold open-mouth kiss, his tongue exploring, making contact with hers. *Enough of the tease,* he thought. He boosted her up in his arms, ready to go to the next level. Her legs automatically wrapped around his waist. Her arms went around his neck. He carried her to the bed where he stretched out over her as she lay on her back.

She put her hands on his chest to put an immediate halt to his intent. "Wait! What about Office Ballard?"

"He can't watch," Chris said and kissed her.

Again, she pushed on his chest. "No, I'm serious. What if he suspects something?"

Chris smiled. "We'll have to be quick—and quiet."

He hoped she wasn't a screamer like his last girlfriend, the sharpshooter he had met at the gun range.

He wasted no time pulling the T-shirt over her head, exposing her bare breasts. He lowered his head so that he could take her nipples into his mouth while he cupped the firmness of each breast in his hand. Like the shirt, her bikini panties were in his way. He tugged them down over her hips and yanked them off her ankles, tossing them into the air. His arousal was building to a point where he had to do something about it. But first, he wanted to drink in her beauty. Lying in total nakedness, she seemed so vulnerable. He would soon claim her, but he wanted to embrace the brief moment before their relationship would be changed forever. In her eyes, he could see the same longing he felt, no hint of uncertainty.

He liked the way her sexy eyes stayed on him. He liked her slight smile, teasing him, tempting him. She said softly, "I can't wait to feel you inside me."

He had to almost tear off the zipper to find relief from the tight confines of his jeans. Using one hand, he spread her legs apart and found that she was fully aroused and wet. At last, he straddled her and penetrated her deeply. He intended to savor every moment, but when she wrapped her legs around him, he came in an explosion that was ten times better than his horny mind had imagined.

He pulled up to watch the expression on her face as she bit her lower lip and moaned with pleasure. He collapsed into a puddle of euphoria at her side. His skin was so damp, he didn't pull her into his arms, but reached over to take her hand in his.

"Megan, I—"

She turned on her side facing him and pressed her fingertips against his lips. "Shhh, don't spoil this moment."

What she said pleased him. He didn't know what he was going to say anyway. Yeah, he had broken a cardinal rule by sleeping with a person involved in an investigation. But he had no regrets. It felt right. More than right, it felt like he had healed an emotional void deep inside, a longing that could only be filled by intimacy with a woman.

While Megan went into the bathroom, he propped himself up in bed against two fat pillows to reflect on what had just happened. He'd always heard once the genie was out of the bottle, you can't put it back in. *Screw the job, my career.* If Nick knew what he was doing two doors down from their room, he could expect an ass-chewing that would take the rest of the night. *But hey, didn't the guy say to make nice with Megan Moore?* And he was so much more than nice.

She came out with the bathroom light at her back, her shapely curves silhouetted as she made her way back to bed. From the floor she picked up her T-shirt and slipped it on, leaving off her panties. She stretched across the bed to kiss him. "You better go. Officer Ballard might think something…well, you know."

His hand palmed her bare ass. With a grin, he said, "Are you worried about my job or your reputation?"

"Both," she said, smiling back. "Please go, Chris. Although I prefer that you stay all night."

"Me, too."

While he was getting dressed, she said, "How was your conference call with the FBI?"

"It went good. As expected."

"How many snipers will there be?"

Her words stopped him cold. When he resumed zipping up his jeans, he said, "Megan, please don't—"

"Just promise you'll do what you can to protect him, to make sure they don't shoot him."

"Baby, I can't promise that. Nick and I are not in charge. We'll be following orders."

She grew quiet. After he lowered himself onto the edge of the mattress, he slipped into his shoes and then turned to face her. With his hand stroking her thigh, he said, "I better go. Besides the cop outside, we both need to get some sleep. We have to meet the team at five."

With a playful smile, she said, "I like the way you apologize, detective."

"Stick with me, honey, and there'll be plenty of makeup sex. My mouth gets me in trouble a lot." He leaned forward to kiss her one last time. "Gotta go. Sweet dreams."

On his way out, he mumbled a goodnight to Officer Ballard but refused to look him in the eye. He didn't want to give himself away. If the Asheville cop was at all observant, he'd detect his just-got-laid look. But before he got away, he felt the officer's hand on his arm.

"Everything alright in there?" Ballard asked.

"Yeah, everything's great. She's going to bed now. We have to leave at five."

"Don't worry. She's in good hands."

Chris secretly laughed at the irony of that.

CHAPTER TWENTY-TWO

*I*t never fails, Chris thought after the fact. *Try to be very, very quiet and you'll bump into a wall in the dark and make enough racket to violate a noise ordinance.* That's what happened when he went into the hotel room where Nick had already been asleep. Chris heard a familiar sound and knew that his partner had just taken the safety off his weapon. Chris simultaneously flicked on the light and called out Nick's name.

"Oh it's you," Nick said, pointing the gun at him.

Chris held out his hand like a traffic cop. "Will you put that thing away?"

Nick put the safety back on his .45 Smith and Wesson, then laid the gun down on the carpet beside his bed.

"That must have been some apology," Nick said as he lay back down and shielded his eyes from the light.

"Well, I had to convince her."

The room got quiet, then Nick said, "I don't even want to know."

As Chris started to undress, he asked, "How's Jennifer? Everything okay?"

"Yeah. She just wanted to know when we're coming back. I guess that's up to Briggs not us. I hope he plays nice and not hardball."

For Megan's sake, Chris hoped so too.

§

Too late to make the evening news, Jared's note was found at eleven-fifteen. A member of the fire department went back to the fire chief's car to retrieve equipment from the trunk and spotted the envelope under the windshield wiper blade. Calhoun got the call and was on site at eleven-forty. He grunted after he read the hastily-written note with the attached letter to America.

"He's mocking us," he said, handing both to another agent. "Showing up here, daring us to catch him. The son of a bitch! And if his threat to turn it up a notch is real, then we need to find him ASAP." Calhoun scanned the faces of the men who had circled around him. Ten agents, all raring to go and put an end to the guy's rampage. "Okay, he came from outside this perimeter from any direction. See what businesses have surveillance cameras. We know he left the note sometime between five and eleven. So canvas the area. We'll break it down into grids, two blocks out." He made assignments in teams of two covering all directions. Before the group dispersed he shoved his hands in his pockets and said, "Somebody somewhere saw something."

The "somebody somewhere" jargon was his mantra, and when he said it a few agents had the nerve to snicker. He didn't give a damn. It always got them moving, busting their balls to get results.

Calhoun paced back and forth, jacked up on caffeine and nicotine. For him, the waiting for any news was torture. As he stared mindlessly at the blown-apart store, he got a call from Agent Taylor with an update about the planned raid to arrest Sam Briggs. Half-heartedly, he offered any assistance if needed. But in truth, he had his hands full in Charlotte with the investigation of the sniper shooting and the explosion at Coleman's.

About an hour later, he got word of a sighting of a suspicious-looking character that had vanished into thin air. Other than that, he was batting zero until the fire investigator came over with startling news.

"Your guy didn't do this," he said to Calhoun. "This was an accident. Propane tanks stored in a contained shed with no ventilation. With the build-up of heat, they exploded the minute the door was opened by someone most likely smoking a cigarette. We found a body burned to a crisp nearby."

"Are you sure?"

"Not one hundred percent, but yeah, it looks that way."

"So the son of a bitch takes credit for something he didn't do?"

The fire inspector smiled and shrugged. "Hey, he wants to be legendary."

CHAPTER TWENTY-THREE

It was almost midnight when the forbidden boyfriend of a sixteen-year-old girl suggested they go skinny dipping. The blonde girl gave a nervous laugh and said, "What would my parents say?"

"They'll never know, baby."

"I don't think it's such a good idea. The water's so dark, and I don't know what's under there. I'm sure it's gotta be cold."

They stood on the widest expanse of a sturdy limb that bowed low over the lake. For her, even venturing out onto the oak tree was daring enough.

"Hey, it'll be fine," he said. "I'll go first and then you jump in—right into my arms."

"I don't know about this," she said, shaking her head.

He squeezed her cheeks between his hands and laughed, mocking her reservations. "Look, I do it all the time. I know this water, and there's nothing under there. No Loch Ness monster, no snakes, no gators. Once you get used to it, it'll be fun. I'll put you on my back and spin you around. How's that?"

"No. I'm not doing it."

"It's not the water that scares you. You don't want to get naked!" He laughed. "No big deal. Watch me, baby."

Her eyes widened and her mouth gaped open as she watched the boy with the build of a competitive swimmer whip his T-shirt over his head and then unzip his shorts. Down to his boxers, he kicked off his sneakers and looked up at her. He waited for her to pull off her own clothes.

"What are you waiting for? Don't be such a wuss."

"I just need some time to... You go first. Don't wait for me."

"Be that way, then." With his back to her, the boy pulled his boxers down over his hips and kicked them away. He jumped into the dark water, making enough of a splash to get the girl wet. Her shock at being mooned turned into a fit of giggles.

She waited for his head to pop up, but only bubbles came to the surface. Almost in a state of panic, she strained in the darkness for some sign of him. Seconds went by, and then his head shot up like a rocket. He let out a blood-curling scream. Then he went under again. There were more bubbles, a longer wait. An agonizing stretch of time and still no sight of him. She tried to stay balanced on the thick branch, a difficult feat since her legs were shaking and she feared losing her footing. Slowly she eased farther out over the lake to search the dark water. At last, he surfaced. In relief, she exhaled deeply, but then she saw his face was contorted in pain. He gasped for breath and swallowed water. He flailed his arms at his side. His head jerked backwards, and for a moment she wondered if he would go under once again. He was sinking, his eyes closing. Was he losing consciousness? Succumbing to the water? Being swallowed up? Drowning? She cried out to him and then whispered, "Please God, please save him." Suddenly his eyes flickered open. As if by sheer will, his head bobbed and stayed above the surface.

"What's happening?" she screamed out.

He opened his mouth as though to answer, but he was only gasping for breath. He finally gained his momentum and lurched forward. He used his arms to tread water and then to paddle his way back to the tree limb. It seemed to her that his legs were like dead weight.

Is he paralyzed? Why doesn't he do a frog-kick to get here faster?

She got down on her knees and stretched her arm out as far over the water as she dared. At last he reached her and with her help, he pulled himself up and lay exhausted across the rough bark.

"My foot," he said through clenched teeth. "My foot." He pointed at it.

She examined it and saw that it flopped downward. A large bump appeared as if it might puncture through the skin. A bone? Broken in two? She couldn't imagine what had happened.

"Talk to me!" she yelled at him.

He squeezed his eyes shut. The severe intensity of the pain was evident on his face. "There's something...something under there," he said. "My foot hit...something hard. It's broken."

"We have to get help!"

She attempted to call 9-1-1 from both their cell phones but could not get a reception. The disadvantage of being so far from civilization, she lamented.

He propped himself up enough to examine his foot. "Can't walk. Go for help."

The thought of going off in the dark by herself terrified her. She would be forced to make the steep climb up the cliff. If she managed to make it to the top on her own, she'd have to muster enough energy to run through the unfamiliar forest to her home. She'd have to tell her parents there was an emergency. They'd know that she had defied them to sneak off with the boy. And the ramification of her disobedience frightened her as much as going alone for help.

When she hesitated, he yelled, "Go! Hurry! Please—"

§

Two hours later emergency workers and the sheriff's office found the boy naked and passed out, wrapped around the tree trunk, seconds from slipping into the dark water. His foot was swollen and double its normal size, twisted at an odd angle with the toes pointing downward.

It was morning before divers found the cause of his injury. They determined that when he jumped into the water, his foot hit the roof of a submerged truck with enough force to cause a bad break. A special wrecker with an extended cable was brought in and used to haul the vehicle to the surface. It still bore the license plate. The number was in the database of federal and state police. The blue Ford F150 truck was registered to Olivia Eunice Bolten, Jared's mother, who had inherited the vehicle upon the death of her husband.

When Special Agent Calhoun was notified that the getaway vehicle had been located, he was jubilant. He said to his assistant, "I told you that son of a bitch had abandoned the truck and was headed for the mountains. Of course now it seems he's back in the Charlotte area. That's fine by me. I don't have to travel."

"There's more, sir," the field agent said.

"What's that?"

"We found gas receipts, sales receipts for materials that could make a homemade bomb, and a shipping receipt for ammo. Bolten made it easy for us. All of it has been preserved in a sealed plastic bag in the glove compartment. Still dry." He handed an object to Calhoun. "And we found this."

"What is it?" With disgust, Calhoun examined the blackish, waterlogged object in the palm of his hand.

"We found it underneath the front seat. Scuffed up, but it looks like a leather band or bracelet like the ones sold at motorcycle shops. The lettering is wearing off, but it looks like it spells out *exterminator*. That's my guess. Maybe that's his nickname."

"Well I've got worse things to call that bastard."

CHAPTER TWENTY-FOUR

DAY THREE - JULY 6, 2014

Cold shower, strong coffee, eye drops. Anything Chris could find to shock himself into wakefulness. Four-thirty AM. He got maybe four hours of shuteye. He'd made it back to the room around eleven after making love to Megan.

Damn! What have I done? Screwed my career, that's what.

Chris braced himself for a profanity-laced chewing-out when he accidentally bumped into his partner as they got ready to head out. At first, Nick kept quiet, only giving him a certain look that said more than words.

"Was she worth it?"

"What's that?" Chris said.

"You heard me, asshole. Was she worth screwing over your career?"

"Don't start, Nick."

"I knew you had a thing for her. All you had to do was wait for this case to be over and then go for it. But no. You had to dip your wick before she was cleared as a suspect. You're an idiot, Lagoni."

"So you're gonna write me up?"

Nick's silence made Chris wonder if his partner would follow protocol and cover his own butt by turning him in to Internal Affairs. Although Chris didn't want to admit it, his actions had put Nick's job on the line, too.

"I'm done anyway," Chris said. "Calhoun will make sure of it. And you know what, Nick? I don't give a shit. So hell yeah she was worth it."

"Have a nice life working security at Wal-Mart, partner."

"Fuck you, Pulaski."

"Whatever. Let's get your girl and get on the road. They're waiting for us."

After they added the finishing touches to their wardrobe, guns and shields, they walked out together.

§

Before Chris had a chance to collect Megan from her room, an FBI agent had already escorted her outside. He saw her standing beside the van that would take them to the staging area a quarter of a mile from the house where Briggs was believed to be hiding. An agent, carrying a cardboard tray full of Styrofoam cups with steaming coffee, handed one to her. Before boarding the vehicle, the team made small talk and joked around like it was just another day at the office. Their breaths were a white vapor in the cool darkness. In the mountains, even summer mornings held a chill until the sun showed itself over the peaks. An overnight rainstorm had left the air pregnant with moisture.

Although Chris and Megan exchanged looks, they didn't speak to one another. He knew she was smart enough to keep their intimate relationship under wraps. He noted that she was shivering and hoped it was just from the cool dampness and not because she was scared. When he watched an agent drape his field jacket over her shoulders, he masked his displeasure. She smiled at the guy and thanked him, avoiding any eye contact with Chris. He had to repress a strong desire to walk over and put his arm around her.

With the help of an agent's extended hand, Megan climbed into the van. She sat in the back with the agent whose jacket provided her warmth. Chris sat in the second seat behind the driver with Nick at his side. No one spoke during the twenty-minute ride over an asphalt ribbon of twists and turns that took them farther into the mountains, deeper into the forest. Finally they reached the staging area. It was a parking lot of an abandoned motel down a twisty gravel road with only a small sign to claim its existence. Despite its shabbiness, it had a gorgeous view of the river thirty feet down a sloping hill. The gravel lot out front was filled with crabgrass, weeds, potholes, empty beer cans, and used condoms. *If anyone thought police work was glamorous, this scene would set them straight,* Chris thought.

He looked on as Megan stood beside the van, watching the agents getting geared up with Kevlar vests, helmets, padding, and guns. He saw the fear in her eyes. When she looked like she was on the verge of tears, he walked over and pulled her behind the vehicle, out of sight and earshot of everyone.

He placed his hands on her shoulders and kissed her forehead. "Are you okay?"

"I'm scared, Chris. Sam—"

"It'll be okay, baby. It's going to work out."

"I'm going to pray as hard as I can that this ends well."

"Yep, that's the best thing you can do for your friend."

"So you believe in prayer?"

"Of course. And I think the man upstairs must be listening. There have been times I should've been killed, but I wasn't."

"I will pray for you too, Chris."

When he heard the crunch of gravel under boots, Chris released her and stepped back. He swept his arm in a forward motion, gesturing for her to step around to the side of the van. When Special Agent John Taylor saw her, he gave Chris a stern look.

"Lagoni, can I see you for a minute?"

When Chris walked over, Taylor crossed his arms over his chest and said, "Does she understand she has no active role in this? She just sits with the negotiator in case she's needed."

"Yes, sir. I explained that."

"I don't like civilians on scene. Makes me nervous. Anything happens with her, it's on CMPD, not us, got that?"

"Yes, sir. Got it."

"Then take her over to meet the negotiating team in the CNU van."

Chris nodded and walked back to Megan. He led her to the Crisis Negotiations Unit van that included technology and other equipment that made the CMPD SWAT team green with envy. They considered their own van a downgrade from what the feds had.

Despite Taylor's trepidations about Megan's presence, the chief negotiator welcomed her warmly. He had a kind face and in Chris's opinion, he could be anyone's favorite uncle. Chris had heard the man had ten years' experience in negotiations and had a reputation of ending talks peacefully with no need to activate the tactical team.

"We want you to feed us information, Miss Moore," he said. "I'll try to start a dialogue with Mr. Briggs, and we'll need you to tell us what hot-button issues to avoid and what will work. We'll be a team, working together. You'll be able to listen in, but you won't be able to talk directly with him. I'll give you a pad to jot down notes, and we'll add information on a whiteboard for me and my team as things develop."

Chris decided the agent must have picked up on her anxiety because he added, "Don't worry, Miss Moore. These things usually end well. You'll have to trust me. We'll take our time— as long as it takes—to end this as peacefully as we can."

His words seemed to calm her. Before Chris left her in the agent's charge, he gave her hand a little squeeze that secretly meant, *it's going to be okay.* Her forced smile, for his benefit, was his last image of her before the start of the operation.

He waited until she was out of sight before he suited up in a Kevlar vest and strapped on his gun and a belt that held two extra clips of ammo.

As he joined the agents and police officers standing around in the clandestine circle of darkness, Special Agent Taylor said, "Let's do this, guys."

CHAPTER TWENTY-FIVE

Megan knew something was wrong, but she wasn't sure what. The chief negotiator picked up a call on his cell phone and turned away from her. His hushed tone in response to the caller alarmed her.

She heard him say, "Okay then. I'm coming outside and we'll discuss it." When he ended the call, he turned to Megan. "Miss Moore, you stay here. I'll be back in a few minutes. I need to discuss something with Special Agent Taylor. Sit tight, I'll be right back."

Without knowing what was happening, her mind went into overdrive, imagining horrible things like the agents finding Sam dead inside the house. She felt weak with dread. Her heart pounded. When her phone rang in her hand, she jumped.

"Meggie," a low voice said.

"Sam!"

§

Fifteen minutes before the negotiator's phone call, agents flanked the house that was believed to be occupied by Sam Briggs. It was the address in the GPS system in the vehicle driven by Megan. As expected, the one-story house was dark, no lights turned on. Hoping for the element of surprise, they were prepared to storm in if necessary. Three agents in the lead, one carrying a battering ram and another a shield, waited on the front porch. The third agent pounded on the door to announce their presence. No sound from inside. No indications of anyone moving around. Again, the agent used his gloved fists to pound the heavy wooden door. All was quiet. With stealth-like movements, men using mirrors with long extended handles went to every window to get a sighting but didn't see Briggs anywhere.

They broke down the door and entered as a group, shield in front, holding weapons with flashlights attached to gun barrels as they made a sweep of the interior. More agents came behind them. Each room was cleared. Briggs was nowhere to be found. The team leader walked out to report their findings to Taylor.

"There's no basement," he said, "but there's a storage building out back. We found signs that he's been in the house and left recently—within the hour is my guess. There are open food containers, empty liquor bottles and drink cans. We found fresh blood on the kitchen floor that led outside."

"He couldn't have gone far on foot." Taylor hitched his chin toward Megan's Nissan Maxima haphazardly hidden between two bushes. Taylor got on the radio and ordered the activation of a helicopter as well as the K-9 team. After he unwrapped two sticks of gum and stuffed them in his mouth, he said, "Okay, troops, let's flush this guy out of the woods."

§

Chris and Nick watched the latest developments from a distance, giving the agents plenty of room to do their thing. The surprise no-show inside the house made Chris tense. He exchanged a look with Nick, who responded to his telepathic-like message with a shrug.

Chris was eager to help in the search, but Taylor had ordered him and Nick to stand down. Chris wondered if Calhoun had badmouthed him, causing the Asheville special agent to keep them on a tight leash.

When the negotiator strolled over, Chris asked him, "Where's Miss Moore?"

"I told her to wait inside the unit. Taylor doesn't want her to know that Briggs is missing."

"I don't think we should leave her in there alone with Briggs missing," Chris said.

"Yeah, I agree," Nick chimed in.

"I'm going to check on her," Chris said, walking away before the agent could stop him.

If Briggs was hiding nearby, Chris knew the crunch of gravel under his boots would disclose his presence. But his focus was solely on Megan and reaching her as soon as possible. He sprinted toward the CNU mobile unit, thankful that the sun was now up and giving enough light to weave his way through low-hanging limbs of pine trees.

Once there, he knocked, but walked in before there was a response. He didn't see Megan in the front section where the monitors and computers were on tables, so he stepped into the back, which was partitioned off by a thin wall and doorway. He knew at once that it was the negotiating team's domain with a computer, telephone equipment, multiple sets of earphones, and a whiteboard with Sam's name written on it. He expected to see Megan sitting in one of the three chairs, but she wasn't there. Calling her name, he rushed out to see if she was around the backside of the unit. Out of the corner of his eye, he saw Nick and the negotiator rushing over.

"She's gone!" he shouted to them as they approached.

"Aw, shit!" Nick exclaimed. "Not again!"

CHAPTER TWENTY-SIX

A rookie agent fresh out of the FBI Academy knocked gingerly on Calhoun's office door. In a gruff voice, Calhoun ordered him to come in. Agent Matt McGinnis stood in front of the desk as if waiting for permission to speak.

"This better be important," Calhoun said. He'd just gotten word from Taylor that Briggs was not in the house as expected.

"It is, sir," McGinnis said. "A man just walked in, and he claims to know the whereabouts of Jared Bolten."

"Is he credible?"

"Yes, I believe so. He seems to have firsthand knowledge. He claims his ex-girlfriend is Jared's sister."

Calhoun, lost in thought, tugged at the starchy collar of his dress shirt. He turned his focus back to McGinnis and said, "Put him in Interview Room One. Set up the video recorder, and get the team together."

Twenty minutes later, Calhoun entered the room where the man was told to wait. He noted that the man's leg moved up and down under the table, causing the side of his work boot to hit the metal leg of the chair. Calhoun wondered if he had been sitting on information for two days, working up the courage to come forward. While the man was left alone, he had finished drinking the water given to him and had crushed the plastic bottle as flat as a slice of bread.

After introducing himself to Mickey Dexter, Calhoun said, "I understand you have some information that would be helpful to our case."

"Yup, that's right. I sure do," Mickey said with a nod. "Is there a reward offered?"

"Yes, we listed a reward on our website, but before we pay out, we have to make sure the information is reliable."

"Oh, it's reliable alright. I just have one other condition before I tell you what I know."

"What's that, Mr. Dexter?"

"Find my brother. Tell you what—just find his girlfriend. He's been living with her, but I don't know where. We had a little misunderstanding and Sonny took off. I need to find him."

"We're not in the missing persons business, Mr. Dexter, unless the person is a minor."

"You don't have to find him, just get me an address for the girl. Her name is Sarah Jane Brackett. I'll take it from there."

"I can't make any promises. Maybe we can determine Miss Brackett's residency if your information pans out."

"Then we've got ourselves a deal," Mickey said.

"What do you have to tell us?"

Mickey seemed distracted, then said, "What? Oh, yeah, well, it's like this, I know where you can find Jared Bolten."

"Where is that?"

"Make that one more condition. Can I have another bottled water? Damn if I ain't thirsty."

Mickey's toothy smile irritated Calhoun. He didn't like dealing with a redneck who could be wasting his time. Despite his impatience, he nodded and stood up. He opened the door wide enough to pop his head out and holler for McGinnis to bring in two bottles of water.

Mickey continued to work his leg under the table. He drummed his fingers on the tabletop, another thing that annoyed Calhoun. The man's hands were calloused and stained with grease. *Perhaps the hands of a mechanic,* Calhoun thought.

He wondered if Mickey was just nervous, or was he distrustful of the FBI? McInnis had asked to see Mickey's driver's license as a pre-screening. A criminal background check showed that Mickey, also known as Mickey D, had a rap sheet that involved resisting arrest, drunk and disorderly conduct, and simple assault. Calhoun worried that pulling information from the man might be arduous and time consuming. And he was not a patient man.

As soon as McGinnis brought the water into the room, Mickey took a long swig, curling his thick lips around the opening. "Man, that's better," he said after he gulped down half the bottle. "Now like I was saying, I know where Jared Bolten might be hiding. He has a bunker. Can't say he's there, but I'd bet my paycheck he is. It's underground and hidden real good. I've been there once. It's something to see, man. He's got supplies that could last for years. I mean that boy has food, water, beer, booze, and explosives and ammo like you ain't never saw. He has a ventilation system, and there's a scope he uses to check out his surroundings. I think the place might have a trip wire. It could blow up any fool before they ever get close, know what I mean?"

"So where is this place?"

"On his mama's land. Well, actually it was his daddy's place, but his mama moved in and claimed it about the time his daddy got real sick. It's about thirty acres, maybe more."

"We've searched every inch of the property. We didn't find anything like a bunker."

Mickey laughed. "Well you searched every inch but the inch where the bunker is. It's not visible. Hidden real good. Built underneath that dilapidated outbuilding that has two walls still standing. On the other side of the creek. It's covered in brush and vines. Trust me, Agent Calhoun, you wouldn't see it unless you knew it was there."

Calhoun remembered that the K-9 team stopped at the creek. The dog's handler said the canine had lost the scent at the creek bed. He explained that the scent had most likely traveled downstream with the rapid current rippling over the rocks on the shallow bottom.

If what Mickey said was true, Calhoun figured they needed to take the utmost precautions. As soon as he got rid of

Mickey, he'd get the director on the phone and work up a plan. The failure or success of the operation could make or break Calhoun's career. He stood up, thanked Mickey, and escorted him to the door.

"What about that reward and that address I need?"

"We'll be in touch, Mr. Dexter. Just leave your contact information with my assistant."

"One more thing, Mr. Agent. I seen 'im. I seen 'im with my own eyes. 'Course he don't look nothing like what ya'll are showin' on TV. I only recognized him because of his mean-lookin' eyes." Mickey gave him a big grin. "See, I saved the best for last. Y'all better start countin' out that reward money."

CHAPTER TWENTY-SEVEN

Megan trekked through the woods searching for the house where Sam said he was hiding. The wet leaves that had fallen on the ground were slippery under her feet. Sunlight tried to push through the tall trees, but the denseness of the forest made it a dim, foreboding place. Her jeans and knit top felt damp from the moisture of brush and low-lying branches. The air held a stillness and the scent of fresh earth. When she scanned her surroundings, she tripped over a fallen branch and fell forward, breaking her fall with her arms extended and her palms flattened. By the time she stood up, her hands and knees were coated in dark soil. She slapped her hands together to brush them off and kept going.

In a break in the trees, she saw the house Sam had described over the phone. A small structure made of logs with a primitive wooden porch. It looked deserted and unwelcoming. She gulped with apprehension as she walked inside.

She found Sam sitting on the floor near the fireplace. The room smelled of dampness and burned wood. With his back against the wall and his legs spread wide, he looked up at her with a blank expression. One of his pants legs was soaked in blood. His face was slick with perspiration. She could tell that he had not slept in hours, maybe days. The gun in his hand did not deter her from rushing to his side.

On her knees, she leaned over and placed her hand on his shoulder. "Oh, Sam, thank God I found you. You're hurt. How bad?"

He licked parched lips and stared at her with dark angry eyes. "You brought them here? You led the FBI to me? How could you, Megan?"

"I didn't, Sam. They followed me."

He closed his eyes, letting the back of his head hit the wall hard. "I messed up bad. That man. Never meant to—"

"I know, Sam. It was an accident. You got into a fight and the gun went off. We'll tell the police that. It's not as bad as it seems."

Through clenched teeth, he said, "How can you say that? A man is dead! Not just any man. They think he's a military hero. I saw the news. He's going to be buried at Arlington with full military honors. I'm sorry he's dead, but he wasn't what they say, Megan. He cheated me and lots of other guys. We risked our lives and we got nothing in return."

"Sam, we need to get help—for your leg. Show me. I want to see how bad it is."

She started to pull up his pants leg, but he pushed her away with the barrel of his gun. He said, "Stop it! No, it's nothing."

"But you need help. It'll get infected, if it's not already."

He squeezed his eyes shut and winced in pain. A trail of sweat coursed down the side of his face. He swallowed hard and then opened his eyes to look at her.

"Megan, you need to find a way to get to the car. We can make a run for it. Go to Mexico. We'll be safe across the border. I've got cash from my place. It's enough to get us there."

"No, Sam! We're not going on the run. You're going to do the right thing and turn yourself in. There's a detective. A good man, and he'll help you."

"No. Can't do that, Meggie. I won't." He paused and looked directly into her eyes. "If we can't escape, then they'll have to kill me. I'm not going to prison."

"Sam, listen to me—"

He shushed her and tilted his head up. The dark pupils of his eyes danced around as he strained to listen. "What's that?"

"What?"

"That sound." He paused again to focus on a repetitious whirring noise. She was troubled by the wildness in his eyes.

Megan heard it, too. "Sam, it's just a helicopter."

He struggled quickly to his feet, knocking her aside. At the window, he pushed the curtain back with the barrel of the gun. He looked far off until he spotted the helicopter headed their way.

Megan felt a chill go down her spine when she realized the man beside her was not the Sam she knew. In seconds he had transformed before her eyes. He was a solider again and under attack by the enemy. He raised his weapon and pointed it toward the tree line outside the window.

To her disbelief, he shouted, "Lawson! Decker! Get down! T-Man advancing. Twelve o'clock! From that hill. Stay down!" He fired the .38 out the open window. "Guys, air support! Won't be long. Five minutes out."

Megan tugged at his shirt. "Sam—Sam, it's okay. Look at me!" His menacing gaze frightened her. She stepped back, her heart pounding. "Sam—Sam, it's me! Megan. You're not in Afghanistan. You're here. Calm down!"

"Megan!" He looked at her with eyes glazed over. "Cover your head! Cover your arms! A woman can't...not here! Islamic law. Hide! I'll protect you."

"Sam! What are you talking about?"

He pushed her down on the floor. "Stay!"

Back at the window, Sam leaned far out and fired two more shots toward the forest. "Take that, you motherfuckers! We radioed for QRF and they're here—gonna smoke your asses! We'll blow you to smithereens, you Taliban piece of shit!" He stared at the floor behind him, as if seeing something or someone. "Lawson, don't you die on me. Hang on."

He fired again. A blast that made Megan jump. Then another. Once again he pulled the trigger. The gun clicked. He repeated the pull on the trigger. *Click.* Realizing the chamber was empty, he tossed the gun aside.

"Lawson? Decker? Don't you dare die. Damn it, stay with me! Dustoff inbound."

He acknowledged Megan as though she had just walked

in. Slowly he came back from the war, into the present, and dropped to his knees. He released a sorrowful moan, prompting Megan to drape her arms around him.

While he sobbed, she cried softly and whispered, "It's okay, Sam. It's okay."

§

"Shots!" Chris said to Nick.

They took off in the direction of the blast. Hurling over brush and limbs, they sprinted through the forest and didn't stop until they heard voices. In the clearing they spotted a log house surrounded by agents. Chris noted that two agents were preparing to throw a flash bang through the window. He charged forward and stepped between them.

"Stop! What if the woman is in there? Wait!"

The team leader said, "We have our orders."

"She could be a hostage!"

"Her status is suspect, not hostage. Now stand down, detective. Like I said, we have orders."

"Oh, yeah? Well, I've got no orders. I'm going in!"

He rushed past them and hopped onto the porch.

"Hey, come back here!"

Ignoring the command, Chris sprinted inside, worried the agent might throw the flash bang anyway. The explosion Chris braced himself for never happened. He looked around until he saw Megan and Sam kneeling on the floor, her arms around him. Moaning, Sam rocked back and forth on his knees.

Chris heard a rumble coming from outside. It was the engine of the Bearcat, and he knew the team had moved the armored vehicle closer. There was uncertainty in Megan's eyes when she looked up at him. He wondered if she thought he was a threat to Briggs, or maybe she expected him to defuse the volatile situation. He pulled her to her feet and away from Sam.

"Megan, I have to take him." To Briggs, he said, "Sam

Briggs, stand up. Come on, let's go."

Briggs looked at Chris as if he was someone familiar but feared. His eyes widened and then glazed over. He did get to his feet, but his legs were unsteady. His hand trembled. He mumbled something incoherent. Before Chris could cuff him, control him, Briggs stepped back. There was a wildness in his eyes. Worried that Briggs might charge him, Chris drew his weapon and maintained his distance. He was about to order Briggs on his knees when Megan stepped between them.

"No, Chris, no! Something is happening." She didn't bother to explain. She directed her attention exclusively to Sam and said, "What is it? What's wrong, Sam?"

"It's him!"

"Who are you talking about?" she asked.

"The man they call the Exterminator. Right there," he said, pointing at Chris. Briggs appeared fixated on Chris's Kevlar vest, similar to military-issue. Never making eye contact, he said, "I know all about you, Sergeant. I know what you say: Killing hajjis is like spraying for cockroaches that either go belly-up or crawl away until they reassemble somewhere else. That's how you got that nickname and you're proud of it. You're not a soldier. You're a killer!"

Sam's lips quivered with alarm. He gasped. His eyes widened as a new revelation overwhelmed him. He found his voice and said, "My God! You're the man on the news! Bolten! You're the Exterminator!" He stared at Megan for a prolonged time until recognition appeared to kick in. Chris wanted to stop her from reaching for Sam's hand, but it was too late.

She held it tightly and said, "He's coming back, Chris. He's coming out of it. The sounds and the smell of diesel from outside triggered a flashback." She stepped closer to Sam and said in a soft soothing voice, "It's okay, Sam. You're here. It's over now. No need to be afraid." Chris calculated that her prolonged silence was intended to come to terms with what

Briggs had said. "You knew him, Sam? You knew that horrible man, Jared Bolten?"

Chris was relieved when Briggs shook his head. He certainly didn't want Calhoun to be right about a connection between Bolten and Briggs. He'd bet his career and reputation on his belief that the two shooting incidents were unrelated.

Assuming from his silence that Briggs was done talking, Chris wanted to get Megan out of the way so he could escort the prisoner outside, but her stubborn stance kept him at bay. Her eyes, pleading with him to take things slow, made him wait. Briggs squeezed his eyes shut and then blinked as if a switch from delusion to reality had taken place.

His demeanor seemed to confirm the rational Briggs was back. He said, "I never met him, but I saw him in Afghanistan. At the airfield. He brought in a group of insurgents. I remember him glaring at me when he pushed a prisoner toward the plane. Eyes that could cut like a knife. Evil eyes. Scary."

Briggs bowed his head and wiped his eyes. Chris pulled Megan back, away from him.

"Let's go, Briggs," Chris ordered.

In his rush to get inside the house to Megan, all Chris's training had left him. He forgot that Briggs was probably armed. By the time he thought to pat him down, it was too late. Briggs had pulled a .22 from the small of his back. He pointed it at his temple while Megan gasped in horror.

She shouted, "No!"

"Don't you see, Megan? I should have died that day. Not Lawson, not Decker. *Me!* They come to me in my sleep. Different fights. Not the explosion in the tank when we all got blowed up. RPGs incoming. Mortar fire. We're surrounded, and my buddies die again. They die every battle we fight. Over and over and over again. Don't you see? I need to be with them."

Tears ran down his cheeks. His finger slid in position on the trigger.

"No, Sam, you can't." She rushed forward, closer. Chris grabbed her and pulled her back. Determined, she said, "For me, Sam. Please. For me. Don't leave me with this memory. I beg you. I care about you."

His hand trembled as he held the gun to his head. Tears continued to course down his cheeks. He hesitated and seemed to struggle in his choice between life and death. His indecision bought Chris some time to consider his options. None were good and all held risk, especially with Megan's close proximity.

Again Megan pleaded, allowing tears to stream down her face. "Please, Sam. Put the gun down. For me. Do it for me."

Sam squeezed his eyes shut. He brought his arm down and let the gun slip out of his hand. It landed on the floor with a loud thud but did not discharge. After Chris kicked the gun away, he walked up to Sam and at the same time kept Megan back.

"Sam Briggs, you're under arrest for the murder of Gerald Mahoney."

Chris unhooked his handcuffs from his belt and put one loop around Sam's wrist and one on his own. Arresting a one-armed man was a first for him and it created challenges he'd never considered.

Peacefully, Briggs walked out at Chris's side, keeping his head down and not acknowledging the agents who surrounded him. Chris removed the cuffs from his wrist and Sam's and turned the prisoner over to the FBI team. He knew before it was over, Briggs would be back in the custody of CMPD and housed at the Mecklenburg County Detention Center in downtown Charlotte.

He watched a despondent Briggs being led away, still staring down at the ground. All Chris cared about was getting back inside the house to Megan, but before he could go to her, he saw her being led out by an agent. Their eyes met and he saw that hers had pooled with tears. Forgetting his job, his training, and common sense, and even knowing there were eyes on him, he rushed over to take her into his arms. Her shoulders shook beneath his arm as he led her away. In the distance, he saw Nick giving him an approving nod.

"He didn't die. Oh, thank God," she said with a trembling voice.

"No. He's going to be okay, Megan."

Away from the others, Megan placed her hand on Chris's arm and said, "I never heard Sam say anything in there about Jared Bolten, did you?" The look she gave him was as determined as her words.

"Nope, I don't know what he said. He was pretty incoherent to me." A lie that satisfied her. She smiled and squeezed his hand.

What Calhoun doesn't know won't hurt him. The son of a bitch would only make a big deal out of nothing.

CHAPTER TWENTY-EIGHT

Two days earlier Chris had wanted Megan to stop talking. He'd joked about putting duct tape over her mouth. Now he wished she would say something, *anything*. He had no idea what her state of mind was because she seemed numb. She'd been silent since he'd told her she couldn't see Briggs until he was processed for booking, and probably not even then.

"Maybe after his bond hearing. In a day or so," he had said. He didn't tell her that Briggs was taken to the infirmary and then put in isolation on suicide watch.

She had pleaded not with words, but with a certain look that made it hard for him not to give in to her request. Truth be told, it wasn't even his decision to make.

"Sorry, Megan. Sometime soon you can see him. They'll take him to the infirmary first, then he'll be processed. Then visitation with his lawyer—the hearing. All that takes time."

She lowered her head and seemed to accept his explanation. After that she stayed silent, even when he and Nick picked up Lisa's Range Rover at the Asheville police station and drove her back to Charlotte in it. She sat up front with Chris behind the wheel and stared pensively at the passing scenery out the side window.

Back in town, Chris dropped Nick off at CMPD headquarters and then drove Megan home. He got her settled inside, then knocked on Lisa's door to return her car keys.

"Detective, I'm sorry," Lisa said. "I'm sorry for my part. I was just trying to help. Thank God my car didn't get into a wild police chase." She thought about what she'd said and added, "Oh, I don't mean Megan would have tried to outrun the cops. Oh, I'm just thinking out loud and not making sense." She glanced down at the keys in the palm of her hand. "Thanks for returning them. I hope Megan is okay."

"She'll be okay. I'm going back to stay with her for a while."

"Good idea."

Was it? he wondered. He wanted to hold her, console her, but what then? What was the status of their relationship? Was it the real deal or was it unbridled lust? Dare he put his heart out there again? Jamie Jackson broke his heart, not once but twice.

He slipped inside Megan's condo and found her where he had left her, reclining on her sofa. She leaned against a grouping of throw pillows with her legs stretched out on the cushioned seat. Although he knew she was physically and emotionally drained, her beauty stayed intact. When he sat down inches from her feet, she attempted a weak smile. He placed his hand on her shin, feeling the starchy denim material of her jeans. "Do you want anything, Megan?" he asked. "Water? Something to eat?"

"Not now. Just stay with me for now. Please."

"You know I will."

He wanted to say more, but what would *more* be? What could make it all better? Her friend was in jail, preparing to be formally indicted for capital murder. And eventually, she'd have to be interviewed by the prosecutor and may have to face Calhoun, for what he didn't know. Maybe just because the special agent was a prick who wanted to ride in the saddle of a big case for as far as it would carry him.

Chris watched as she closed her eyes. He thought she was drifting off to sleep, but she opened them to gaze at him. She seemed more relaxed than she'd been all day.

"I feel dirty," she said. "I want to get out of these clothes and soak in the tub."

He looked down at her jeans soiled with dirt and Sam's blood from his leg injury.

"Okay. Need any help?"

"What does that mean?"

"I mean, anything I can do? Like fix the water for you. Get some towels. Whatever."

"Oh," she said, "I thought—never mind what I thought."

"Megan, I know what you thought. I'm not insensitive. I know that now's not the time."

He pulled her close. He pressed his lips against her forehead, inhaling her sweet fragrance that in a more opportune moment would have sent him over the edge, kissing her, touching her, making love until morning light.

His decision to stay the night seemed to please Megan. He wouldn't share her bed because it would have been torture. To have her close and not be allowed to touch her because of her emotional state would drive him nuts. He settled for her sofa with memories of another sleepless night from a short time ago. A lot had happened since then. He was supposed to be a cop who knew how to separate his professional from his personal life. But he was also a man whose desires and needs could only be met by a woman.

He had Megan on the brain as he lay on the sofa in his boxers, hugging a pillow to his chest. It was just a guess, but he figured it was around one o'clock in the morning. She was a short walk down the hallway behind a closed door. If he could only have her, then he could succumb to sleep. *Damn, thinking about it doesn't help,* he realized. It only made his desire and insomnia grow stronger.

With his head cradled in his hands as he stared up at a ceiling he couldn't see in the dark, he heard her bedroom door open. Bypassing the living room, she headed for the kitchen. He got up and followed her there. Leaning against the door jamb, he studied her standing at the kitchen counter, unaware of his presence. The frugality of the 15-watt stove light bathed her in enough illumination to reveal the sexiness of her short silk gown. It hugged her hips, showing her curves, and when she turned around, he saw the fullness of her breasts. It would take all the willpower he could muster to keep from carrying her back to bed to make wild passionate love to her.

"Megan, are you okay?"

She gasped, then covered a smile with her fingertips. "You scared me, didn't see you come in," she said. "I couldn't sleep, can't stop thinking about Sam in that jail cell probably scared out of his mind."

"He'll be alright. It's not as bad as you think."

"I hope you're right." She filled a kettle with water. "I decided to make some lavender tea. It's supposed to help with sleep. Do you want any?"

"No thanks. I'm not much of a tea drinker unless it's iced and sweet. A southern thing."

"Yes, I know," she said. "Hmm, I can't reach the box of tea bags. The problem with Sam helping me put up groceries, he always puts things up too high. Do you mind? It's beside the container of rice."

"Sure."

She moved a little to the left to allow him room to reach up. When he turned to hand the box to her, she moved closer. The slight movement made the thin strap of her gown slip off her shoulder and the flimsy material flopped down over her breast. He stared at it as if seeing it for the first time. His fingers slipped underneath the strap and pushed it back in place. When his eyes locked with Megan's, his resolve was weakened, and then defeated. His sudden kiss caught her by surprise, but she responded eagerly to his embrace. His kisses trailed down her neck. He splayed his hands across her ass, squeezing the flesh. His body pressed flat against hers, slipping and sliding on the silk fabric. His hand ventured underneath the hem and his fingers hooked over the waistline of her bikini panties. He felt her hand clamp tight over his.

"Chris—"

"I want you so much, Megan," he whispered.

"Not here."

He took that to mean she wanted him, too. He scooped her up and carried her to bed. He had her gown and his boxers off in a mad rush. Everything about Megan awakened his senses to a new level, so intense he felt he would lose his mind until he had come inside the warm, moist pleasure spot that awaited him. It pleased him that she moaned in ecstasy and clawed his back as she too reached orgasm. When he lifted himself up to gaze at her, he found her eyes closed, her sensual lips curled in a smile.

"You're so beautiful," he whispered.

Falling in love with her would be so easy that he felt it was only a matter of time. He had known her only a few days, but somehow it seemed like she was a part of his life for longer than memory served him. A love destined to be? Maybe. Time would tell, but for now he would take one day at a time. To love someone as passionately as he wanted to love her scared the hell out of him.

CHAPTER TWENTY-NINE
DAY FOUR - JULY 7, 2014

J ared stared at the television and wished he'd heard wrong. The news reporter said that the FBI was now saying that the explosion at Coleman's was an accident. Not an act of terrorism. The note he left on the fire chief's car was a complete waste of time. And worse, he'd exposed his location. *Stupid, stupid, stupid,* he thought as he hit the heel of his hand against his head. It meant that authorities would no longer be thinking he was holed up in the mountains. They'd now concentrate their search in the immediate area. He cursed under his breath for screwing with the plan: to hunker down and wait them out. In his thinking the feds would eventually tire of the search, or at least cut back their efforts. When that happened, he could finally leave his bunker and make a getaway for Mexico. Once there, he'd have a daily ritual: go to some beach somewhere, get high, and get laid. Just thinking about it made him smile.

He'd only stopped by his friend's house for something to eat. He'd eat, drink, and watch a little TV. He wished he could get into the freezer and find a steak that he could thaw out in the microwave. But he was still afraid of opening the freezer lid and having to deal with the gross object on top. Instead he found a can of tuna and pork and beans in the cabinet. While he watched the news, he ate both straight out of the can. He burped and made a sour face from the aftertaste. He hit his chest with his fist and then picked his teeth with a dirty fingernail. Another big belch and fart and he felt better, except for the latest news report that cleared him of involvement in the store explosion.

"Guess I'll just have to show 'em." He made the statement out loud because his daddy had always said, "If you proclaim it out loud, then you really mean it, son."

It was now clear to him that the shooting from the church tower wasn't enough for them to print his letter to America or show his video message. The feds had even taken down his website.

Again out loud, he said, "I need to do something big. Shit, it's gotta be a 9/11 kind of thing if I'm ever gonna get their fucking attention."

Because the bunker was where he did all his serious thinking, he made his way back there. After he hid the motorcycle behind a tree, he climbed down the ladder. He sat on his makeshift bed made from plywood pieces and a thin mattress he got out of a garbage bin behind a dollar store. He stared at the Molotov cocktail that he had carried to Megan Moore's apartment and thought of ways he could still use it. After all, it was good to go; he'd already soaked the rag in gasoline. It would make a huge fireball wherever he decided to throw it, but it had risk. Someone could spot him right before or right after he tossed it. In his opinion, the C-4 explosives might be a better option. They could be set off from a safe distance with a detonator. Besides, it would be expected that an experienced military guy, such as he, would use explosives, and although the Molotov cocktail could do serious damage, it was primitive and amateurish.

He prided himself in being a careful planner and also very meticulous. In a neat row on a table, he'd set out his supplies: Molotov cocktail, blasting caps, hand-rigged detonator, and C-4 blocks, more of the same on the floor underneath. *Tools of the trade*. He laughed at that.

Whatever Jared decided to do required serious thought and careful planning. Otherwise, it would be a FUBAR mission. And nothing, no nothing, must go wrong.

Jared wished he had the luxury of time, but he didn't. Something had to happen sooner rather than later. He had to do it now while his name was in the news. He had become a legend. Hell, he'd heard there were reporters from Great

Britain, Germany, France, and Japan covering the story of his Fourth of July fireworks show. *Those jokers hadn't seen anything yet. Just wait.*

First, he figured he needed to decide where the attack would take place. It had to be somewhere public, with lots of people, easy access, and limited security. A shopping mall would be a prime target. Who in their right mind is scared of a mall cop? They were usually retired patrol officers that had gotten fat, slow, and lazy. No real threat. He knew shopping centers had cameras everywhere, in parking lots and at entrances, but what about loading docks? Near trash bins? Maybe not. A mall was his first choice, and if that didn't pan out, he figured he'd target a high-rise office building. *Nothing on the grand scale of the Twin Towers in New York, but this wasn't fucking New York.*

He stretched out on his bed and closed his eyes, imagining the planned event. The media would have a field day. If anyone on the planet hadn't heard his name yet, they would now. And the candy-ass feds would finally print his letter to America. He'd make a run for Mexico before the cops had time to react. They'd be tripping over themselves while he cruised desolate back country, finding sweet things along the way that would put him up for a night. All he had to do was show his cock and a big smile, and he'd be in the door, drinking their booze and eating their food. *Easy.* It had worked another time he had skipped out on a warrant, the time he had forced himself on Jenny Lynn, and her daddy had called the cops. Eventually the charges were dropped and he came back to town. In his experience, things always managed to work out in the end.

Of course, this was different. He'd never show his face anywhere in the US of A ever again. No problem. He'd make amigos south of the border.

He sat up and reached for a cigarette because he felt more like a smoke than a chaw of tobacco. He lit it and set it on the edge of the table while he stood up to stretch his legs. Reaching for his cell phone, he knocked over the Molotov cocktail. *Shit!* It fell next to the cigarette and the rag stuffed in the bottle's neck flamed up. At a frantic pace, he tried beating the flames out with his bare hands. His hand accidentally sent the glass bottle sailing in the air. All Jared could do was helplessly watch, unable to stop what was about to happen. It shattered into a thousand pieces right on top of a C-4 block and blasting cap.

His last words before the explosion were "Oh fuck!"

§

Minutes earlier... "One down, one to go," Calhoun said to Agent McGinnis as he ended the call with Special Agent Taylor. "They've taken Briggs into custody. Now if they can only get him to talk. Christ, I hope he doesn't lawyer up. We need that guy talking."

They walked side by side with Calhoun feeling every bit the mentor to the junior agent. He knew he had more law enforcement experience than the kid had years on earth. They made their way across Bolten's land to find the dilapidated shed and then the bunker where they hoped to find Jared Bolten holed up. A tactical team fronted them, taking their time to scout for pressure plate explosives or a trip wire. Their IED techs, former marines, were the best in the bureau, and Calhoun had the utmost confidence in their ability to keep the team safe.

The heat of the mid-morning sun caused a layer of perspiration to form on their foreheads and sweat to roll down their necks. Wearing heavy Kevlar vests only made it worse. Walking over the uneven ground with lumps of hard clay and holes that could turn an ankle, Calhoun tugged at his belt. He ran his fingers over the butt of his gun in its holster as if to assure himself that it was there.

He pointed straight ahead. "We go that way. Almost there once we reach the creek. On the other side is the bunker. Won't be long now, McGinnis. This is your first major takedown.

You'll never forget this."

Calhoun grinned like he held a winning lottery ticket. He lived for moments like this. It was as exhilarating as having a good-looking woman on an adjacent barstool writing down her phone number, or better yet, her hotel room number.

Suddenly they felt the earth move beneath their feet like an earthquake, only they weren't anywhere near a fault line. The ear-piercing boom that accompanied the shaking earth was too deafening to be thunder.

"What was that?!" McGinnis shouted as the earth blew up two hundred yards ahead. Clods of dirt and debris rained down in all directions. Flames shot up, sending a mushroom cloud of black smoke into the sky.

The agents stared in disbelief as items burned everywhere they looked. A motorcycle against a tree was burned to a crisp. About fifty yards from the origin of the explosion, an IED tech squatted down to examine something. He stabbed an evidence marker into the ground beside it and left it there, rushing over to Calhoun.

"Body parts," he said, pointing over to it. "Part of a hand." As if the horror of the sight did nothing to faze him, he said with a grin, "I'm almost sure we can get prints off it."

Calhoun was in a state of disbelief. The sour look on his face let others know he was pissed. His gut told him that the body part found and more to come would identify the deceased as Jared Henry Bolten. Although he didn't come right out and say it, he felt cheated out of the pleasure of taking into custody the man who had terrorized the city and killed or injured so many.

Calhoun looked at McGinnis, who gazed at him as if waiting for some noble words of wisdom. All Calhoun could mutter was, "Son of a bitch!"

§

Four hours after Bolten blew up himself, his bunker, and a mountain of evidence, Calhoun and Homeland Security held a joint press conference. Of course, hours earlier the news had been leaked to the media. All major networks had breaking news reports. At the news conference, Calhoun answered whatever questions he could while withholding some key information "pending a full investigation," he told them.

"I'm not at liberty to comment at this time. Next question," he'd say, pointing to another reporter. *Oh, the feeling of power over these media predators.* And there was nothing they could do to trick or intimidate him into saying more than he wanted to say. *Screw you,* he thought anytime some hard-ass reporter said something like, "Sir, you still haven't answered my question. Again, can you tell us?" And blah, blah, blah, they had kept asking away, rephrasing the same damn questions. Vultures, he considered them, although he needed them to give credit where credit was due: the FBI, and of course, under his leadership.

§

After the press conference, all the power players met in the conference room at the FBI field office, including Special Agent Taylor from Asheville, the director of Homeland Security, and representatives of CMPD homicide division. Chris and Nick tried to conjure up an excuse to skip the meeting, but Sergeant Holden insisted that their attendance was mandatory. They sat through a replay of the last three days in which Calhoun never admitted his mistake.

"After questioning Sam Briggs, he denies any connection to Bolten," Calhoun told the group.

Because there wasn't any, asshole, Chris thought.

"It is possible that Briggs entered the area with the intention of taking out specific targets. Colonel Mahoney was not the only military officer standing behind the stage that day. Several other guests, all military, were in the immediate vicinity."

Make it up as you go, you prick.

"With that said, the investigation of the murder of Gerald

Mahoney has been delegated to CMPD and the county prosecutor. Of course, the bureau will be available to offer any assistance. Our focus will be the sniper shooting and subsequent events."

Which is where your full focus should have been in the first place, dickhead. Not trying to muddle our homicide case!

After the meeting, Chris was almost out the door when he heard Calhoun call out to him.

Aw, shit! Chris strolled over, taking his time, his hands in his pockets.

"What?" he asked.

Unaffected by Chris's brusque manner, Calhoun said, "Just want to say no hard feelings. We got into it a couple of times, but hey, emotions run high in cases like this. Are we good?"

Calhoun extended his hand. Chris looked at it and contemplated the peace offering. *What the hell,* he thought. Shaking Calhoun's hand, he said, "Yeah, we're good."

He'd have preferred to slug the guy, but he was in enough trouble with his superiors as it was. Holden wanted him to take paid leave, but Captain Bowers was not as generous. He wanted him suspended indefinitely. He stated that Lagoni had disregarded security measures, allowing a suspect to get away on his watch. And of course, there was his lack of cooperation with the FBI, even walking out in protest during a briefing.

The captain has no problem kissing the FBI's ass, Chris lamented.

"I'm ready to tell them all to take a flying leap," Chris said to Nick. "Calhoun continues to spout his little fairy tales. And they pacify that bastard by listening to all his bullshit. They pretty much threw me under the bus, Nick, especially Bowers. Guess I'm getting a suspension. And I thought we were brothers, we all stick together, but hell no."

"So unfair. I can talk to the sergeant if you like. You're the one who was right all along. You knew Bolten and Briggs were two separate deals. Hell, you tried to tell them."

"Screw them. Screw the job."

"You don't mean that, Chris. Take the damn time and cool off."

"Oh, I'll be taking time off alright, maybe for good."

"And you sure as hell don't mean that." After a long pause, Nick said, "Look, I'm not telling anyone about Megan. As far as I'm concerned, it never happened."

"Doesn't matter. I'm done, Nick. The next time you see me might be on Whitey's boat, and I'll be reeling in a marlin off the coast of St. Some-Fucking-Island."

Nick grimaced. "I don't even want to picture that. You're crazy, you know that?"

Chris shrugged and as he walked away, Nick called out to him. "Where are you going?"

"To see Megan—tell her about my fishing trip."

"You're walking away from her, too?"

"She deserves better than a fucked-up, workalcoholic cop with a short fuse."

"Why don't you let her decide that?" Chris started down the corridor toward the elevator bank. Nick caught his arm. "Lagoni, at least take some time to think about it before you make any rash decisions."

Chris looked at his watch, then back at Nick. "Okay, you're right. Let's get a drink so I can think it over."

"Oh, sure. Alcohol will clear your thinking."

"It won't hurt. You coming or not?"

§

"You've been drinking," Megan said when Chris showed up at her door.

He gave a sheepish grin and shrugged. "I didn't drive drunk if that's what you're thinking. Nick drove. He's actually waiting in the car. I wanted to see you," he said, turning to see where Nick had decided to park.

"Come in," she said, stepping back.

"I called you," she said. "Did you get my message?"

"Yeah, that's good news."

"Yes, thanks for your recommendation of a lawyer. You're right, this guy is good. He told me he thinks the prosecutor will reduce the charge from murder to manslaughter. And I talked to a veteran's organization today. They're going to give Sam some support. Maybe monetary, I'm not sure, but at least counseling. He's finally going to get some help for his PTSD. And I found out the sheriff's office offers group sessions for anger management and job skills."

"That's great, Megan," he said. "Look, can we sit down? I have something I want to say."

"Sure. Do you want something to drink? Black coffee, maybe?"

He smiled. "Hey, I'm not that drunk."

As he followed her over to the sofa, she said, "Why were you drinking?"

"Because I'm messed up. I don't know what I want."

They sat down side by side, his leg touching hers. "You'll sort it out," she said.

"Yeah." He reached over and took her hand in his. "That's why I'm going away for a while. To sort it all out."

"Going away?" She raised a brow and sucked in her bottom lip. "Well, I hope your *break from life* will help you figure it all out."

Her sarcasm stopped him cold. He ran his thumb over her hand. "I'm sensing some weird vibes here. Are you pissed at me?"

"Why would you think that? You show up intoxicated, tell me you're leaving, and you don't know what you want." She looked directly into his eyes. "Does that include me, Chris? You don't know if you want me?"

"I want you so much it scares me," he said. His comment was followed by silence. He cleared his throat and added, "When you figure out that I'm a first class asshole, you'll want out. And you will, baby, believe me. I'm a cop, and I don't know how to be anything else."

"You don't give either of us enough credit. I can live with you being a cop. We've been through a lot together the last couple of days. As a matter of fact, I saw a side of you I didn't particularly like. But I also saw a loving, caring man. For me, it wasn't just a few romps in the sack, Chris. You're in my system now, like it or not."

He ran his hand over his face, then placed it on her bare thigh, liking the feel of her soft skin. "You say that now, Megan, but wait until I'm missing in action. When I work a case, that's it. I have no private life. I won't do that to you. You deserve better."

"Are you saying the job comes first?"

He hesitated while he searched for what he wanted to say. *Nick was right,* he decided. Alcohol was not the best solution for clear thinking. Finally, he said, "I'm saying I'm not sure the job and a relationship will mix. They're not compatible. I'll hurt you, and then you'll hurt me back. That's how it always works out in my life. Before that happens, let's put this on hold."

"Regardless of how I feel?"

"You might feel different in a few weeks. A break will help both of us. I can't even think straight when I'm around you." Again, he reached for her hand. "I need time away to sort it out. If I still want to be a cop, can we have a future together?"

He thought of a past relationship that unraveled when he chose work over love. By the time he had realized his mistake, it was too late. From her pissed-off look, he knew he had disappointed her. He braced himself for what she would say.

"You remind me of crime scene tape," she said. "Like it's wrapped around you, barring all others from entrance. *Keep Back—Do Not Enter.* Well, I get the message loud and clear. You guard your heart and don't let anyone near it."

"Megan, that's not what—"

"Save it, Chris. You should go. Don't keep Nick waiting any longer."

"I'm leaving in the morning for Calabash. When I get there, I'll call. Maybe by then you won't be so pissed at me. I'm not intentionally trying to hurt you, Megan."

"No, don't call. Not until you've *sorted it all out.* So go on to Cala—Cala-hooch or wherever-in-hell you said you're going."

She turned her head away to wipe at her eyes and then stood up. "I'll walk you out."

At the open door, he paused to place his hand under her chin and force her to look at him. "Please try to understand—I have to be sure what's best."

Although she was upset, she let him kiss her. *It lacked passion, but at least it was something,* he thought. He looked out at Nick sitting behind the wheel of the car and then turned back to her.

"Take care, Megan. I'll see you when I get back—in about two weeks."

After she closed the door, practically in his face, he feared she would start crying. He'd noticed tears pooling up when he made her look up at him. Walking back to the car, he felt like shit. He was an asshole, and the last five minutes had proved it. Better she know now rather than later, he decided. By tomorrow, he'd be out on Whitey's boat with a beer in one hand and a rod and reel in the other. And Megan would again be involved in creating a report with crunched numbers that made sense only to some corporate bigwig. Life would go on.

CHAPTER THIRTY
DAY FIVE - JULY 8, 2014

Mickey Dexter studied the paper on which Special Agent Calhoun's assistant had written down the address of Sarah Jane Brackett, his brother's girlfriend. The FBI had come through with that as promised. He had yet to see any reward money, but they did determine where he could find the woman and hopefully his brother. It was a no-brainer to expect to find Sonny living off another woman like he did from time to time when he didn't have steady work. From what he'd heard, his brother had been laid off from a construction job a few months back.

When he drove up to the address written on the paper, he didn't see Sonny's motorcycle out front, just a black Honda Civic. Probably belonged to Sarah Jane, he reasoned.

He adjusted his ball cap and coughed nervously before he knocked. It had been six months since he'd seen Sonny. They'd had a big brawl over money owed, but Sonny couldn't remember if he owed Sonny money or if it was the other way around. Once they would cash their Friday paychecks, they shuffled money around like cards.

The purpose of seeing his brother was to make peace. He missed doing things with his little brother, like going to bars, watching NASCAR races, rabbit hunting, deer hunting, tinkering around with motorcycles and cars.

A short blonde with big tits answered the door. *Her makeup's a little on the heavy side for my taste, but damned if Sonny didn't do good with this one,* he thought. She gave him a once-over as if wondering who he was and why he was there.

"Hi, are you Sarah Jane?"

"Who wants to know?"

He gulped when she spread her feet wide to block entrance into her dumpy little house.

Okay, Sarah Jane, don't want to be friends? No problem.

"My name is Mickey Dexter. I'm looking for my brother, Sonny. I heard he was staying with you."

"Got that right. He *was* staying here. I kicked him out a month ago."

"So where can I find him?"

She cocked her head to one side and hesitated. "You sure you're his brother?"

"Of course I'm sure! I wouldn't lie about that." *Bitch!*

"Well, he's staying at a house on Rankin Street the last I heard. If you don't find him there, I hear he's working at Murray Motors. Finally making some money, not that it does *me* any damn good. He owes me about a grand in back rent, not to mention all the groceries I fed that guy."

"Can you write the address down? Maybe Sonny will pay you back. I'll ask him."

"Like that's gonna happen," she said, rolling her eyes. "C'mon in, I'll write it down for you."

Twenty minutes later, Mickey arrived at a house that looked abandoned. *When was the last time somebody cut the grass,* he wondered. He stepped up onto the front stoop and knocked. There was no answer, and he didn't see Sonny's motorcycle anywhere around either. He found that the front door was unlocked, so he walked into a room that looked like Sonny thought garbage belonged on the floor. He almost tripped over an empty can of tuna and another that had contained beans. *Still a slob, I see,* Mickey thought. He sniffed the air, wondering about a foul odor he picked up as he moved toward the kitchen. It reminded him of the spoiled beef burrito he'd found in his truck two days after he left it there, decaying in the hot sun. He discovered a sink full of dirty dishes, some with dried, caked-on food remnants. A trail of ants marched in a zigzag from the floor to the countertop.

He walked through the rest of the house, calling Sonny's name. With no sign of his brother, he wandered out to the garage, thinking Sonny might be out there messing around with some motor parts or something else. He found it almost as messy as the house with tools scattered about on a table made from a door and a pair of sawhorses. A grease spot on the concrete flooring showed where a vehicle had once been parked. With his thumbs hooked over his belt, he scanned the windowless perimeter and unfinished walls exposing the wooden frame and Tyvec siding.

What looked like a new Whirlpool freezer caught his eye. He chuckled. Sonny always said he'd get a big-ass freezer to put his game in. Now he'd done it. *Good for him.* The time he shot a deer, they had to give most of the meat away because they had no place to store it.

"Would ya lookee here?" Mickey said out loud as he admired it. "Man, oh, man."

His curiosity got the better of him. He decided to lift the lid and see if his brother had stocked it full of game. He pulled the string on the naked light bulb in the center of the garage to get a better look at what Sonny had bagged. The latch on the top was a little tricky, but Mickey figured it out. An ominous creaking sound sent a shiver down his back, although he didn't know why he felt spooked. Until—

He couldn't believe what he saw. *No, it couldn't be. No, no, no—NO!*

He jumped back, repulsed by what lay on the very top in a clear plastic bag. After another look, confirming it was true, he fell to his knees, shaking, trembling, and sobbing. His hand shook so badly he couldn't steady his finger to press 9-1-1 on his cell phone.

§

Now that the fun part was over—being interviewed, press conferences, a one-on-one video call with the director— Calhoun had to get down to the nitty-gritty grind of filling out reports. He had to document the full operation for posterity. The deceased Jared Henry Bolten was now a case study. He would be studied and talked about for years to come by profilers, psychologists, law enforcement everywhere. Another example of an active shooter for the training academy. There'd be more, Calhoun knew. As long as there were guns and mentally unstable individuals, there would be more shootings, more deaths. The opening of schools throughout the country after summer break would mean the beginning of "open season," as he called it. There'd be innocent victims who did nothing to deserve such an unexpected, violent death. *Sadly, no end in sight,* he lamented.

He was deep in the drudgery of such a report, when Agent McGinnis tapped on his open office door. Showing irritation with a scowl, he looked up at the junior agent.

"What is it, McGinnis?"

"Sir, Bolten had twenty-one confirmed kills in that shooting, right?"

Calhoun pushed back his chair and ran his hand over his bald head. "What's your point?"

"Now it's twenty-two, sir. He killed twenty-two individuals."

Calhoun closed his eyes and exhaled. "Don't tell me that little girl in the ICU died."

"No, in fact, they say she's going to make it."

"Then what in the hell are you talking about?"

"I just spoke with the sheriff of Gaston County. They found a body."

"What's that got to do with Bolten? He's dead. You can't kill anyone if you're dead."

"You can if you kill the person days or weeks before you

die. They found a Popsicle in a freezer. Bolten's prints were all over the place. And get this, the motorcycle—that burned-up Harley—we found at the bunker site was registered to the man they found. Maybe Bolten killed the guy to steal his bike."

"I'll be damned," Calhoun said. "So that was his new mode of transportation. He dumped the truck and was getting around on that Harley. I should have given the guy more credit. Have they notified the next of kin?"

"The brother found him, sir. Here's the thing—the brother is Mickey Dexter. We gave him the address for that woman and she led him to the house where Sonny Dexter was found."

"Damn! We helped Mickey find his brother, but not the way he wanted it."

"No, sir. He wanted it to be a happy reunion."

"Well, it didn't turn out that way."

"No, sir. It sure didn't."

CHAPTER THIRTY-ONE
DAY TEN - JULY 13, 2014

Megan was nervous. She had been to see Sam only one time before, but she hadn't adjusted to the process of visiting someone in jail. She had to go through a metal detector, show her ID, allow herself to be patted down. Once she got the all-clear, she waited in a closed-in booth for Sam to show up and pick up the telephone so they could converse through a glass panel.

When he entered she noticed that his hair was disheveled, in need of a cut. His eyes looked tired as if he hadn't slept. His orange uniform, too tight for his beefy six-two frame, had short sleeves that showed his stub. She remembered that he liked his sleeves longer so it was completely covered.

He barely managed a smile. "You look good, Megan."

"Thanks, but what about you, Sam? Are you okay?"

"I'm existing," he said and paused to study her face. "Don't worry, I'll be okay. They're going to put me through some tests. Psychological stuff. Then I might go in with the general population. They have a common area where the inmates share showers and bathrooms. My luxury suite will be a thing of the past," he said with a chuckle that seemed artificial and only meant to put her at ease. "It scares me some, but I guess I can take care of myself. They better not say anything about my..." He stopped and looked down where his left arm should have been. "I almost died to get that badge of honor."

"Sam, I want to ask you about something."

"It must be important, you look so serious."

"The letters," she said, pausing to gauge his reaction. "The love letters you wrote to me, but never gave me. The police found them."

He squeezed his eyes tight and shook his head. "You weren't ever suppose to know about them. They had no right!"

"Don't be angry, Sam. It's okay. I just want you to know I had no idea you felt that way."

"Yes, but what good does it do? You don't feel the same. You're probably repulsed because I'm not a whole man."

"Now *I'm* angry!" she said, raising her voice. "You know I'm not like that. I just want to be friends, Sam. Can't we just be friends?"

"Yeah—just friends. I accept that."

"Do you?"

"What other choice do I have? Besides, I wouldn't want you or any woman waiting for me while I'm locked up."

"This could be a good thing, Sam. Now you'll get some help. People *do* care. You have to believe that."

He nodded and smiled. "I do believe that. Don't worry, Megan, I'll get through this, and I'll be stronger for it."

What he said warmed her heart. He sounded more hopeful than he had at any time since his injuries. She left him, feeling like a load had been lifted from her shoulders.

Walking toward the parking garage, she felt the heat of the afternoon sun rise from the sidewalk. She was glad she chose light linen pants and a short-sleeved cotton blouse to deal with the heat and humidity. It was the most conservative thing in her closet. Sam's lawyer had advised her to tone down her dress when visiting the jail. He explained it was necessary because of the inmates' stares and catcalls.

At the crosswalk, she waited for the light to change. On the opposite corner, the sight of a familiar figure made her heart quicken. Chris! Or was it? Same muscular build, same height, same confident swagger, but still she wasn't sure. Behind his baseball cap and sunglasses, it could be him. At last, the walk signal indicated it was okay to cross and she rushed across the street. When she got closer, she realized it was not Chris. Behind the darkness of his sunglasses, she could tell the man gave her careful scrutiny and smiled appreciatively. With the push of the crowd, their bodies almost touched, but he continued going toward town as she headed in the opposite direction toward her parked car.

The beat of her heart went back to its steady pace. The few seconds of elation took a dive. It had only been a few days since she had told Chris goodbye, but it seemed like time had arduously dragged by. Her cell phone rang and without looking at the screen, she picked it up and said, "Chris?" She immediately felt foolish for making the assumption, but thoughts about him still lingered.

"No, it's Nick. I was just calling to see if you'd heard from him."

"No, I haven't. Is everything okay?"

"Sure, sure. It's just that we're trying to get in touch with him, and he doesn't pick up his calls."

"Oh, no."

"Hey, don't worry. I didn't mean to upset you. He's okay, Megan. He'll call. We'll hear from him when he wants us to. I know the guy. As stubborn as they get. A jackass, but hey, gotta love 'im."

§

In Chris's opinion, "the good life," as Whitey called it, didn't live up to the hype. It was supposed to be idyllic days of fishing, riding the waves in a big-ass boat, hot girls in bikinis, fresh seafood fried to a golden brown, and bars right on the beach with big-name bands.

Whitey forgot to tell Chris that their days started at five in the morning, cutting up bait, fueling the boat, and getting everything ready for the charter groups. He also forgot to mention the brutality of weather, either blazing hot and humid or raining hard enough to stir up the ocean with eight-foot swells that made Chris seasick and puke over the side. He saw no bikini-clad ladies, only middle-aged women in too-tight shorts and tops with their fat threatening to burst out like toothpaste out of its tube. And the local bars had no bands. They were farther south in Myrtle Beach, where the real night-life heated up the action.

Damn Whitey. That lying son of a bitch.

Chris left Whitey on the dock still cleaning fish for their day's guests while he went to get a cool one in the nearest bar he could find. The trouble was he didn't see any place that served his purpose. He got in his car and drove across the state line into South Carolina. He wound up in an open-air bar and grill right on the docks at Little River. A Bob Marley song played over the speakers while customers sat on high bar stools around tall circular tables or at the counter. But no matter where they parked their derriere, they had a good view of the boats coming in from a day out on the water.

"I'll have a Stella," Chris told the bartender as he took a seat at one of the round tables.

The beefy guy with spiked hair the color of wheat hollered to his assistant. "Hey, Rocky, pour a Stella for the FNG."

Chris wasn't looking for a fight, but whatever the dude had called him didn't sound right. "What did you call me?"

The bartender met Chris's gaze and then diverted his attention to the view over the water. "Don't worry about it. It was nothing."

"No, I want to know." Chris gave him a look that let the guy know even if he was dismissing the remark, Chris wasn't.

"It's a military term, that's all—means Fucking New Guy. I didn't mean any harm. You're new to fishing, and I picked up on that."

"How do you know that?"

"Well, let's see. You're sunburned, you smell of fish, and you've got no battle scars from hooks on your hands or arms. But I see you've got a bandage there on your thumb from not knowing the proper technique of unhooking your catch."

Chris smiled. "Not sure I'm cut out for this."

The bartender grinned. "You'll find out soon enough once the cooler weather sets in. It's a whole different crowd down here. Serious fishermen and serious weather."

Once Chris was served his beer, the bartender sauntered away to greet two locals. While the trio laughed and joked, Chris sipped his beer and stared out at the water. A charter boat had just glided in with its fishing poles secured in brackets on both sides of the boat, sticking up like bamboo shoots. As the passengers disembarked, Chris observed that they looked sunburned and tired from their day out on the water. It was similar to the scene when Whitey docked his boat. The vacationers held up a string of fish or opened a cooler with their catch on ice to show family and friends there to greet them. He took it all in as he sat alone. Alone and pathetic, his self-proclaimed analysis of himself. No one there to share a drink, the sunset, or small talk.

But he had no one to blame but himself. He chose to leave everything behind to explore the possibility of a new chapter in his life in a new place. He was lost in his thoughts when he thought he heard his name called. He looked to his right to see a familiar face.

"Chris! Wow, imagine seeing you here."

It was a pretty blonde he had dated for a brief time in Charlotte. She had dumped him when his police work had gotten in the way of their relationship. She had especially hated his last minute calls to cancel a date. When he was a no-show at a rock concert he had forgotten, she had left with someone else. When he had called to apologize, she told him he was out and the new guy was in.

"Heather, good to see you." *She's put on weight.* "You look great."

"Thanks, you do too. Why aren't you out looking for bad guys?" she teased.

"Taking a little break. Can I buy you a drink?"

"Sure. I'll have what you're having."

When she pulled up the bar stool beside his, Chris motioned to the bartender, pointing to his drink and holding up two fingers. He noticed that her hair was blonder, maybe bleached. Besides her weight gain, he noticed her heavy makeup, which made her appear older than she was. He thought of Megan who used a light application to enhance her beauty.

By the time Chris had started on his third beer, Heather had gotten him caught up on her life since their split. It included two marriages, a baby, and four moves. Always a talker, he was content to just listen, revealing little information about himself.

She set down her empty beer bottle and said, "So, I decided to take a long weekend down here since my ex has our little girl for a few days. And that's about it. I'm a single mom, moving back to Charlotte and starting a new job." She placed her hand on his arm and said, "Maybe we could get together once I get settled in."

He was taken aback by her salacious gaze and sexy smile. A red polished nail ran down his bicep. If it was intended to reignite a spark that had faded long ago, it failed miserably. However, had it been Megan's touch, a charge would have shot through his body like lightening. He sensed a toughness about Heather that he surmised was the result of two bad marriages and subsequent divorces. He thought she was trying a little too hard to reconnect. Maybe she expected to pick up where they had left off eight years ago.

Chris didn't like women who appeared desperate. Megan had won him over easily and simply by her compassion, her intelligence, and her independence. Not only was Heather so unlike Megan, he found her presence unsettling. He'd finish his beer and tell her he had to be somewhere. As if there was some damn truth to his statement.

She cocked her head to the side and gave him another playful smile. "What is it, Chris? Is there someone else?"

"Yeah."

She frowned. "Where is she? I'd love to meet her."

"In Charlotte."

"I see." He thought she did an admirable job of masking her disappointment with a big grin as though she was happy for him. "She must be special."

He couldn't help his smile. "She is."

Heather bit down on her lip and stared out at the water. When she turned back to face him, she gave him a poignant stare and said, "She's one lucky lady."

"No, I'm the lucky one."

She placed the strap of her handbag over her shoulder and slid off the bar stool. As she pushed her hair away from her neck, she said, "I have to go now. It's good to see you, Chris."

He watched her walk away, headed in the direction of another bar. Having a beer with Heather had a sobering effect, a moment of clarity. He finally understood what he wanted, no longer unsure whether to continue on the police force and/ or pursue a relationship with Megan. He wanted both. And he wouldn't let another hour, minute, or second go to waste.

As fast as he could, he scratched off in his car and made his way back to Calabash to gather up his gear and tell Whitey he was leaving. In half an hour, he was on the road headed west.

§

Chris made the long trip back to Charlotte in record time, breaking speed limits along the way, coasting through red lights in fly-by-night towns when he sensed no watchful eyes of police. He pulled up in front of Megan's condo around one in the morning. At such an ungodly hour, he figured she would be asleep. Knocking on her door and scaring her was not an option. Instead, he called her.

It took five rings before she answered her cell phone. "Megan?"

Her voice was thick with grogginess. "Yes?"

"Megan, it's me. Chris."

"Oh," she said, lacking the enthusiasm he'd hoped for. "Why are you calling? What time is it?"

"I know it's late, but can I come in?"

"I thought you were at the coast?"

"No, not anymore. I'm outside your door." His statement was met with silence. "Hello? Are you still there?"

"Yes, I'm here."

"Well, will you let me in?"

She made him wait before she said, "Have you sorted it all out?"

"My life? Yes. I know what I want."

"Oh, yeah? What's that?"

"Just come to the door, Megan."

He heard the phone click. A wait that lasted only seconds but seemed much longer gave him a feeling of uncertainty. *Is she coming or not,* he wondered. The door creaked open. He looked up to see Megan in a sexy nightshirt, deep pink and silky. It looked as if she had quickly run a brush through her hair before she came to the door. She placed her hand on her hip and shifted her weight from one foot to the other.

"You said you sorted it all out, so what do you want, Chris?"

"I want you, Megan," he said. "I want us."

He'd hoped she would looked pleased, maybe smile, and rush into his arms. Instead she stepped back to give him room to enter. She ran her hand through her hair and walked away from him. Halfway to the kitchen, she turned to face him and said, "I'm fixing some tea. I'll get you some coffee."

With her back to him, she stood at the counter putting the kettle on the stovetop and pouring coffee and water into the coffeemaker. As she waited, she tapped her fingernails on the granite surface. Chris pressed against her and placed his hands on her shoulders. He kissed the back of her neck, inhaling a sweet fragrance he had become accustomed to.

"I missed you," he said softly.

She turned her head sideways. "I missed you too."

"Then what's wrong, Megan?"

She turned around in the tight space between them. As he searched her eyes for some meaning, he ran his hands up and down her arms.

"We need to talk, Chris."

He cast his eyes down. "I hurt you, didn't I?"

There wouldn't be the joyous homecoming he had imagined. She wasn't about to rush into his arms or lead him to her bed. No, he would have to work his way back into her life, back into her heart. His soul-searching journey had become his undoing.

She didn't reply to his question. Words would not find their way past her lips until she sat across from him at the small table where they had once shared a pizza, a time when neither trusted the other.

"You left so suddenly, so unexpectedly," she said. "That's what hurt me most. I needed you, Chris. I was hurting because of what we went through together and hurting, too, for Sam. You just left! Why? I know what you said: You didn't know what you wanted. We needed time away from each other to make sure." She pressed her lips together and stirred honey into her hot tea. "I think you ran from a commitment instead of running toward it."

"Guilty as charged." He reached for her hands and held them tight in the center of the table. He studied her gaze, then said, "You're right, Megan. I was scared because I found myself falling in love with you and it seemed too soon, too rushed. I didn't want to trust what I felt. But when I was away I found out that I want you more than anything in the world."

As they talked, time slipped by without notice. Long after their move from the table and to the living room sofa, they stayed close, bodies touching, holding hands, debating a future neither pretended to comprehend. They came to an agreement, a mutual understanding of a strong attraction, a heartfelt bond neither could deny.

"I never stopped thinking about you, Megan. My heart ached for you. I want you so much," Chris said as he hugged her tight, his lips at her ear.

She placed her hands on the sides of his face and kissed him, lightly at first, but then deeply. He pulled her tighter, closer, feeling her strong heartbeat against his chest. He picked her up and carried her to her bed, leaving only the dim light from the hallway to guide him. He helped her out of her silky nightshirt. His fingers worked their way inside her panties and forced them down where they got tangled around her ankles. She laughed as she kicked them away. His eyes stayed on her as she lay on crisp white sheets and he frantically stripped off his shirt, shorts, and boxers. He covered her body with his own, kissing her hungrily. Her quick breaths showed her arousal as his lips traveled down her neck, her chest, her breasts. She moaned when his fingers found their way into her erogenous zone, so wet and ready for him. When he penetrated her, he felt his climax building, ready to explode. The momentum built with each thrusts until he came with a mind-blowing release. Megan's orgasm lasted longer, leaving her limp in his arms.

Their long discussion and lovemaking took most of the night. As sunlight spilled into the room, Chris awoke and rubbed his eyes. He turned his head to see Megan at his side, still naked with the bed-sheet twisted about her body, one leg and arm protruding out. Slowly and carefully, he got up, hoping not to disturb her. He slipped into his boxers and made his way into the bathroom and then the kitchen. He wasn't sure if Megan even drank coffee but he put enough in the coffeemaker for them both. To his delight, a search of her fridge led to a discovery of the makings for breakfast: a carton of eggs and bacon. He found a loaf of bread and a toaster on the countertop.

By the time she was up, he had everything set out on the

table. She said the smell of bacon frying made her get up.

Holding a crisp strip between her fingers, she took a bite and smiled. "You are so sweet to do this, Chris."

"My pleasure. I wanted to surprise you."

He took a sip of coffee. Everything about the moment felt right. He wanted more mornings like this with the sunlight coming in through the window and washing across Megan's beautiful face.

When his phone made a few beeps, he pulled it from his pocket to see who could be sending him a text message. He looked at the screen and said, "Damn."

"What is it?" Megan asked.

"It's Nick. He wants me to call him, says it's important. I turned off my ringer so I guess he couldn't reach me. It better not be about work. I still have another week on my suspension."

"What do you think it's about?"

"I don't have a clue."

Nick's text that demanded a phone call from Chris turned out to be good news. When he returned to the kitchen, he sat down across from Megan at the table. He took a sip of coffee that had gone cold. Before he spoke, he laughed and shook his head.

"You won't believe it," he said, deliberately making her wait.

"What is it?"

"Nick's a daddy! Jennifer gave birth an hour ago. A girl. Can you imagine Nick with a little girl?" He laughed. "She wasn't due for another two or three weeks."

"That's wonderful news. We'll have to visit them once they get settled in at home."

§

A week passed before Chris and Megan stopped by to meet the newest member of the Pulaski family. Nick lead them down the hallway to the nursery and stopped in front of the crib.

"Megan, Chris, meet Caitlyn Elizabeth Pulaski. Isn't she a beauty? Takes after her mother."

"Thank God," Chris teased. "She's a little doll. So tiny. Look at those little fingers," he said as she balled up her fist and placed it on her ruddy cheek.

"I wish she'd open her eyes for you," Jennifer said. "She just went to sleep. She won't be awake for another four hours and then she'll scream for her next feeding."

"I can't help with that," Nick said. "That's mama's job."

While Jennifer and Megan stayed inside to chat, Nick directed Chris outback. They settled into the comfort of matching chaise lounges with the convenience of cup holders if they decided to set down their cans of Coors Light. The seating arrangement overlooked the freshly mowed lawn, which Nick had done that morning before the heat of the day set in. Nick said it was a good time to sit outside because the position of the late afternoon sun put it behind the large oak tree, giving them plenty of shade. As they sat there, Barkley bounced over with a ball in his mouth, ready to play. After Nick threw it out into the center of the yard, the dog took off.

"Everything is changing for us. Personally and professionally," he said, turning his attention from Barkley to Chris.

"Yep, I guess so. You have a baby and a new promotion. By the way, congratulations, Sergeant. I'm sorry I missed the presentation."

"No big deal. Holden said a few words and then you know the Cap. Wouldn't stop talking. Major Lackey finally had to pull rank and shut 'im up." Chris laughed at that, imagining the scene. "Which reminds me, Lackey said you're being reassigned to a special task force. What's that about?"

"They have a drug kingpin setting up a network in the city and whacking some of his lieutenants. I'll actually be working with the DEA on the operation. Can you believe that?"

"But you hate working with the feds."

Chris smiled and took a sip of his beer. "That may be true of the FBI, but not DEA. I get along fine with those guys. I'm going to Quantico for a briefing and some additional training. I'll be gone for about two weeks. Long time to be away now that I have a new woman in my life."

"So you really like this one?"

"Yeah. So what do you think? Do you like her? I mean, do you like her for me?"

"Hey, I'm not giving you any more advice about your love life. We're not partners anymore so I'm off the hook." He tried to look serious, but failed with a grin. "Megan is looking good for you now that she's no longer a suspect."

"Megan was *always* looking good."

They shared a laugh. "You got that right."

Barkley ran up to Chris instead of Nick, nudging his leg with his nose as he held the ball in his mouth. Chris threw it farther out than Nick, and the dog scrambled away.

"That could go on all night," Nick said. "He doesn't get tired. As long as you throw that ball, he'll go get it."

"Hey, we're both having a good time," Chris said as he watched Barkley snatch up the ball and head back toward them. "Nick, guess what? Megan wants me to meet her parents. I've never met parents so early in a relationship. That scares the shit out of me."

Nick laughed. "You're okay with hardened criminals, but a girl's parents scare the shit out of you?"

"Maybe they won't like me."

"They'll like you, dumbass. They'll see how much you care about their daughter, and you'll be in. You'll get the parent stamp of approval."

"I hope so."

They heard the door open and saw Megan stepping out to join them. As always, Chris was captivated by her enticing green eyes and sexy smile. She walked over to him and eased down to sit at his side. He sat up straighter and reached over to rub her arm affectionately.

She said, "I hate to break this up, but Chris, we have dinner reservations at seven. Shouldn't we be going?"

He glanced at his watch and nodded. "Yep, you're right. Traffic is bad at this time."

"Dinner reservations?" Nick said with an arched brow. "If he's taking you to a place that requires reservations, then you've added some class to this ol' boy, Megan. You should see some of the dives he likes to hang out in."

"My taste has improved," Chris said, looking at Megan to insinuate that she was the cause and effect. He swung his leg off the lounge chair and stood up to leave, grabbing Megan's hand and pulling her up too.

After one last look at the baby sleeping in her crib, Megan and Chris said their goodbyes. Chris started the car and reached for Megan's hand, squeezing it gently. "You're the best thing that's happened to me in a long time."

Smiling, she said, "Is that so, detective? I say ditto to that."

"Miss Moore, why weren't you that agreeable when I first met you?"

"Because you were playing bad cop to offset Nick's good cop routine. Remember?"

"At the time, I thought you were a spoiled, high-maintenance woman who was holding back on key information."

"So your opinion of me has changed, detective?"

"You could say that," Chris said, leaning over for another kiss.